Purrfectly Bound

A MAVERICK PRIDE TALE

C.D. GORRI

Purrfectly Bound:
A Maverick Pride Tale #6
by C.D. Gorri
Edited by BookNookNuts

Copyright 2022 C.D. Gorri

To my purrfect readers,
enjoy.

Before you begin sign up for my newsletter here:

https://www.cdgorri.com/newsletter

Blurb

The youngest Honor Guard in the Maverick Pride is about to lose his stripes…

Lance Jacosa has spent his youth working his way through the females of Maverick Point, but something is wrong, and the young stud has lost his mojo. He needs help—*the professional kind.*

It's a good thing Uncle Uzzi is coming down to Maverick Point for a visit—even better when Lance discovers the old Witch has the Tiger Shifter's mate with him.

Annalia Reese has agreed to accept help from her neighbor, the owner of a matchmaking service, but can she trust the elderly man's claims that supernatural creatures exist? Even crazier, Uncle Uzzi swears Shifters love curvy girls!

Will a plus-sized human take on a guy with a Tiger-sized crush?

Find out in Purrfectly Bound.

Preface

Uncle Uzzi was just on his way back from a whirlwind romance he'd helped set up in a small village in the south of France when he felt an unmistakable pull to visit one of his homes in the Northeastern United States.

He hit the call button as he lounged in the main sitting area of his private jet and waited for the pilot to answer.

"Captain Charles?"

"Yes, sir, Mr. Stregovich, what can I do for you?"

"Now Charles, you know you should call me Uncle Uzzi," he began. His magic began buzzing anxiously, but Charles was quick to acquiesce.

"Apologies, Uncle Uzzi," the Eagle Shifter replied,

and Uzzi's magic settled at the comfortable tone of his voice.

"That's alright. Now, I know we had plans to go to California, but business is calling me back to Burlington County, any chance you can get me to Maverick Point?" Uncle Uzzi asked.

"Let me see," Charles said, and came back a few moments later with good news. "There is a small private landing strip owned by the Devlin brothers in nearby Barvale, New Jersey. We can be there in six hours. Will that work, sir?"

"Yes, yes, that is fine. I will call my driver to meet us there. Thank you, Charles."

"My pleasure, sir, *er*, Uncle Uzzi."

Uzzi hummed softly, allowing his muses and energies to flow freely. Yes, he was definitely needed in Maverick Point. But a stopover at the little condo he'd bought himself in Barvale seemed just the thing.

He picked up his phone and shot off a message to Hank, his honorary nephew, and favorite limo driver, telling him to meet him there at one o'clock that afternoon. Meanwhile, he would close his eyes and see if he didn't get any visions of his darling *liebling* while he rested.

"We've got another job with our favorite pussycats, liebling. I feel something very special in the air," he whispered, knowing wherever she was, his sweet Betty would be pleased.

Looks like another purrfect match is on its way...

Prologue

"I'm so done with this shit, Lance!" The female stormed out of the connecting bathroom to his room at the Pride house.

Brenda grabbed the slinky little dress she'd worn earlier that night, tugging it over her semi-naked body. He'd known the she-Tiger since high school, and they'd enjoyed a *friends with benefits* relationship on and off for the past five years.

He grimaced as she slammed the door, rattling the framed autographed posters of some of his favorite football players he'd hung on the wall. Fuck. He felt like shit and didn't blame her for being pissed.

Five years of no strings sex and this was the first

time he'd ever failed to rise to the occasion. It sucked balls she was one of the Pride, someone he'd once sowed his oats with back in the day. Word of his *problem* was bound to spread like wildfire, and Lance so did not want to deal with that shit.

"Brenda, I told you, I'm just tired—"

"Yeah, right. You are *tired*, Lance. Maybe you should see a doctor," she snarled before walking across the room to find her shoes.

"Fuck," he growled, shaking his head.

He couldn't even drum up enough interest to feel bad. As for his Tiger, if anything the beast was relieved the overbearing female was gone. He wanted none of the she-Cat's attentions, and Lance could not blame him.

Lately, she'd been coming on strong, hinting about claiming bites and having cubs. His balls just about crawled inside him when she'd mentioned seeing Doc Mikey about going off her birth control for her upcoming heat cycle.

Fuck no.

He wanted no part of that. Fathering her cubs was not something he saw himself doing. Besides, he had nothing to offer the skinny female. And he'd told her so, repeatedly. A loveless match like his parents had just didn't appeal.

Could anyone blame him? He'd had a front-row seat the past couple years, witnessing every single one of the Neta's Honor Guard find their fated mates. It was a miracle, er, not really. A crafty old Witch named Uncle Uzzi had brought this string of good luck to the Pride. Him and his Magical Match-making Service.

Everyone was constantly begging their Nari, Elissa, to call the elderly man to set up an appointment. He had to admit, he'd been thinking about it himself lately.

That's why he was surprised when Brenda had asked him to sire her cubs. The she-Cat was not for him. She wasn't his fated mate—a hard truth his Tiger recognized and telling her had been difficult.

Slowly, Lance rubbed his hand over his face. He'd been trying to stay awake, but he was wiped out between work and dealing with this load of crap. Brenda had known from the start what the deal was, and she had never had issue till now.

He was more than fine ending their arrangement, but now he had to deal with the fallout of her rumor mongering. Like it was his fault his dick decided to take a nap despite her striptease.

Fuck.

What time was it anyway? He had work tomorrow, and the Nari had asked him to take her to her OB/GYN appointment. His Tiger chuffed and rolled his eyes at the thought of him, an elite member of the Neta's Honor Guard, chauffeuring the man's mate to her *lady doctor* appointment.

Oh joy, oh fucking rapture.

He was a fan of Elissa's, but the Nari had to know he was already breaking out in hives at the thought of that detail. But maybe it was better than hanging around and listening to whatever poison Brenda spread around about him.

He really didn't understand her at all. He'd told Brenda he was tired, had all but stopped seeing her the past few weeks, but she insisted on coming over last night after he'd run into her at *Bar None*. The place used to be a dive bar, but with a new owner, it had turned into a veritable hotspot located in nearby Barvale.

Lance and Brenda had a few rounds of drinks, and she insisted on catching a ride with him. He'd offered to drive her home, but she wanted a nightcap, so, gentleman that he was, he'd offered her a beer. Too tired to drive again, he told her she was welcome to stay the night.

But that was all he offered. No sex. Just sleep.

Lance did not touch the female except maybe with his leg when he laid down on his bed. It was his fucking bed, after all. If she wanted to sleep beside him, then fine, but it had to be strictly platonic. It was the only way his Tiger would allow her to stay.

The beast had gotten territorial and downright picky. He did not want Lance fucking around with just anyone, and yes, it put a huge cramp in his style. Fucker would not let him get laid, and it was all he could do to keep his skin.

"Look, Brenda, I'm trying to sleep. What's the matter?" he asked.

"Are you fucking kidding me?" she asked and growled. "Whose underwear is this, Lance? Is this why you won't sleep with me? I found it tucked inside the face towel, for shit's sake."

The long-legged female tossed a purple thong in his face, but for the life of him, he had no idea whose it was. How was a guy supposed to remember a thing like that, anyway?

Wait—did she say it was in his face towel? Gross.

"Brenda, I don't know what the hell you're talking about," he grunted and sat up, tossing the panties into the trash bin. "First, I live in the Pride House. Those panties could belong to any of the females here—we share a laundry room. But even if we didn't, you and me, we ain't a couple. We are not dating, *or fucking*, or anything at all. Not for weeks!"

"How can you talk to me like that?" she asked.

Fuck him, it looked like she was about to start with the waterworks.

"Like what, Brenda? We've known each other a long time and I never lied to you or pretended feelings I did not have. Hell, I don't even think you like me!"

"But you asked me to come here—"

"No. I didn't. *You* invited yourself here. It wasn't the other way around," he answered firmly.

Yes, it was shitty. But she better face facts now. Before she went real nuts and smashed his cell phone or something.

"Fine," she snarled, and he noticed the tears were miraculously gone. "What can I say? I thought you were special, but you're not," she huffed, tugging on her heels.

"I'm sorry if you made this out to be something it wasn't, Brenda. I am sure you will find someone who makes you happy—"

"Oh, fuck you, pal! You know something else, Lance? You'll get yours," she growled then spat at him.

Holy fuck. Classy.

Lance dodged her loogie and frowned at it as the she-Cat slammed the door to his room and stormed out of the Pride House.

Well, shit.

Chapter One

T hat hadn't gone well at all. His Tiger snarled angrily as Lance looked for some cleaning wipes to pick her spit up off his floor. Who did that? Yuck.

His Cat didn't give a fuck about the she-Tiger's tantrum. She was not theirs, and besides, he'd been a gentleman, Treated her respectfully. Paid for the drinks, drove her home, and he hadn't laid a paw on her.

What would be the point? His beast had lost interest in chasing tail some months ago. It was hell to admit. A man had his reputation to think about, after all.

Sure, he'd tried a little kissing and cuddling, but even that seemed to send his beast into a rage. He had nothing left in him for the females of the Pride. Lance had to face the truth. He was fucking broken.

Physical contact used to be the only thing that worked to soothe his anxious Tiger, but lately it wasn't enough. His ornery Cat rejected any attempt at physical contact with the women in the Pride.

Lance had no fucking idea how to deal with any of this shit. Typically, the single Pride females enjoyed going out with him. He always told them right off the bat that he was not looking for anything permanent. When he took a woman out, it was as friends, and maybe if they both consented, they could have a little fun. Usually, they were okay with the arrangement.

But Brenda changed recently, or maybe she just never really believed him when he said theirs was a no strings deal. He tried to go over the events of the night and was astounded.

They'd had fun shooting whiskey and playing darts at *Bar None*. He felt relaxed and happy when he drove back home. Sure, it was odd she wanted to stay after he'd rebuffed her attempts to touch him and kiss him at the bar, but he'd shrugged it off. They were friends. Friends could have sleepovers.

Of course, he should have known she was gonna start some shit when she'd stripped off her dress and gotten into bed. It was obvious she was expecting something, but he'd just turned around and tried to go to sleep—*exactly like he'd told her he was going to.*

The purple thong, though? That was news to him. He had no idea who'd slipped the purple underwear in his room. Could have been a laundry mishap, but it was more likely one of the other unmated Tigers living in the Pride House was playing a stupid prank.

Assholes.

He shook his head and got up to take a shower. Might as well get some reps in if he was going to be awake, anyway.

The sound of crying cubs caught his attention, and Lance grinned. The Maverick Pride House was crawling with tiny bundles of joy.

Literally.

The little cuties were everywhere. At first, having so many young around had scared the wits out of a confirmed bachelor like Lance. But then he'd changed his mind. His Tiger yearned for a cub of his own, even as his human side scoffed and denied it.

Brenda wanted cubs.

Not Brenda, his inner Tiger snarled.

Lance exhaled a deep breath and dressed quickly. He'd been plagued by the constant hearted yowling of his beast every freaking time he heard the tiny, precious cubs moving around the Pride House.

Okay, fuck the reps.

Uncle Lance was going to pass by the nursery, see if he could help the Nari with the little ones.

Yes, his animal replied. His Tiger liked that plan. Unsurprisingly, by the time he got there, the Nari was already inside with her two twin girls, Melly, and Celia. Her bestie, Jessica, was there as well.

The redheaded female was the Pride leader's sister. Hunter Maverick, Neta of the Maverick Pride, was a good man. He'd raised his sister, Jessica, from the time she was a teenager.

The female had grown into a fine Tiger, mated now to the Pride Beta, a Black Bear Shifter they sort of adopted from the neighboring town of Barvale. Of course, Brayden was a huge mountain of a man and something of a badass.

He loved his mate fiercely and was an excellent second to their Neta. Jessica stood cuddling her newborn cub, a sweet boy named after his father for some dumb reason.

Why call him Brayden when Lance was a perfectly acceptable and available name?

"Morning, ladies," he said, grinning widely at the two mothers. "How are our precious cubs today?"

The females stopped their conversations and turned to face him.

Uh oh.

Lance knew when he was in trouble. Elissa rolled her eyes at him and shook her head in disappointment. The Nari lifted Celia, patting the toddler's back gently and gave him the kiss of death—she *tsked* at him.

"You are in so much trouble now," Jessica whispered, and gave a very unladylike snort.

"What? What did I do?" he asked, pointing at himself.

Fuuckk. Were all the ladies in the Pride going to hate on him today?

"Let's see. What did you start with? Oh, yeah. *Good morning.* Is it, Lance? Is it really a *good* morning? Huh, sport?" Jess asked.

"Um, is this a trick question?"

"You tell us," the Nari snarled, then relented her angry stance. "Okay, look. You're young and unattached. We get it. You have certain *carnal needs*—"

"Um, Nari? Please stop—" Lance gulped. He tried interrupting the woman, but when she was on a roll, there was simply nothing doing.

"Now, we ain't mad at ya. We both know you're

all *Mr. Playa-playa*, but we heard Brenda leave before. She was not exactly quiet," the Nari informed him.

"Yup," Jessica added, emphasis on the *p*.

Elissa narrowed her eyes at him. She lay Celia down inside the crib and lifted Melly, deftly changing her morning diaper, and pulling some soft, fuzzy, pink looking outfit on the precious babe.

Lance wondered how she did that without even looking. It was like some intense mom sixth-sense shit or something. He didn't know, but damn, it was cool.

"Shi—*darn*," he growled, and cleared his throat. "Nari, I apologize for that. If she slammed the front door, or was rude, I am so very sorry."

"Yeah, well, that is not all, buddy," Elissa said. "You know girls talk to each other, and, well, it seems a lot of your dates lately are *less than happy*," she continued, to his utter horror.

"Now, if you need advice, on you know, *boinking*," Jessica piped in and to help, she inserted her index finger into a hole she made using her opposite hand.

Fucking fabulous.

"We can get our mates to talk to you. Brayden has got the best moves," Jessica finished, a wistful expression on her face, but Lance was already covering his ears.

"Hunter too. You know, he does this thing with his hips," Elissa confided, grinning as she whisper-growled and started wiggling her booty. "Like wiggle, swerve, then slam home, baby—and yowza, he takes me there every single time!"

"Oh fuck. Gods, please stop talking," he shouted.

Lance averted his gaze, baring his throat respectfully. He loved these females, would protect them with his life, but there was no fucking way he wanted any part of a conversation like that with the two of them.

Elissa and Jess looked at each other then back at him. But Lance was still trying to clear those horrifying images out of his head.

The Nari held sway over the Pride—maybe not to the extent of her mate, the Neta, but she was pretty fucking strong in his humble opinion. When she was angry, watch out. Lance did his best not to cross either of these fiercely protective females.

"Hey, if it ain't that, then what's the problem, dude?" she asked.

"Maybe we should call him *dud*? I'm just saying, you know, until his dangly bits are back in working order," Jessica whispered.

"Hey, be nice," Lance told Jessica with a frown. "My dangly bits are perfectly fine. I swear to you both. Yes, Brenda was pissed, but only because I would not have sex with her last night. I did not do a thing wrong," he explained.

"She said it was because you had some ho-bag's clothes in your room before her—" Jessica told him unhelpfully.

"What? No! I was out last night, not with any female. One of the guys left that underwear in my place as a prank, but it does not matter. Brenda is not and never was my girlfriend," he hissed.

"So, you just use the Pride females for quickies without shame?" Elissa asked.

"Come on, Liss, Jessi-cat? You know me better than this," he mumbled, hurt by their characterization of his honor. "Brenda and I were never exclusive, even when we were dating. It's been over for weeks now. Last night was not a date. We just happened to be at the same place and were hanging out. She wanted to come back here, so I took her. But nothing happened. No nooky. I promise and I don't know who's purple thong that was in my room, I just figured one of the guys was punking me."

"Shit," Elissa bit her lip and looked around. Was it him, or did she look just a little bit guilty?

"What?" Jessica asked.

"Yes, Nari, what?" Lance asked and picked up baby Melly. The tiny beauty was giggling at him as he started gently tickling her tummy.

She was such a sweet cub, even when she drooled all over him. He didn't mind one bit. Both twins were talking and crawling too, like little speed demons.

Melly and Celia were perfect angels, as far as he was concerned. Just cherubs. It had touched him greatly when Elissa started calling him Uncle Lance.

He'd vowed then and there to do everything in his power to help protect them. He adored all the cubs in the Pride. Perhaps that was why he'd just recently started fantasizing having some of his own.

The problem was, Lance did not have a mate. Far as he knew, no one in the Pride belonged to him. It was a sad, lonely feeling. Everyone seemed to find their other halves—*except him.*

"Alright, I confess. Hunter and I might have gotten a little freaky in the laundry room on one of the Pride cleaning days, I don't know, last week or something." She cleared her throat, but nothing could contain her scarlet blush.

"OMG! You nympho!" Jess snorted again, jostling baby Brayden, who let out a loud cry. "But how'd your panties wind up in Lance's laundry?"

"How should I know?" Elissa shrugged. "I was busy."

"Busy gettin' busy," Jessica added with a little shake of her hips.

"Like you and Brayden haven't broken damn near every piece of furniture in your bedroom. All I did was lose my panties!"

Lance wished the floor would open up and swallow him whole. The last thing he wanted to hear about was these two females' sex life, for fuck's sake. He cleared his throat and put baby Melly back in her playpen.

"Okay ladies, I think I've heard enough," he began, attempting to leave the room.

"Oh, I don't think so," Elissa growled. "Sit down. Panties aside, Lance, I think it's time you stopped being such a rounder. Especially with our Pride ladies."

"Mmm hmm," Jess pursed her lips.

"Uh—" Lance allowed himself to be shoved into a chair, but even his Tiger winced when both females stood in front of him.

"You're not as young as you used to be. You're starting to gray at the temples."

"What?"

No way. He was not gray. He was barely thirty-five, for fuck's sake. Elissa raked him over with a steely gaze that made him cringe.

Fucking hell.

He was about to get the mother of all lectures, wasn't he? Okay. Lance was man enough to go through it. However, the tentative knock on the door, and the subsequent entrance of both Hunter and Brayden, had him doubting his resolve.

"What's going on in here?" the giant Black Bear Shifter asked, bending down to retrieve his newborn son and give his mate a gentle nuzzle.

"Elissa." Hunter's eyes flashed gold with his Tiger as he kissed his Nari on the lips with so much love and emotion, Lance felt like a damn voyeur.

"Hi." The Nari softened as she addressed her mate, "Would you two mind the babies? Jess and I are about to school our Lance here on what needs doing in his life."

"Oh?" Hunter grinned, gold eyes flashing at him for a second before returning to his mate. Lance knew then, without a doubt—he was fucked.

"What might our young Lance here need, my love?"

"I'm thinking he could do with a visit from Uncle Uzzi," Elissa said and smirked at him before glancing mischievously at Hunter.

Oddly enough, along with the healthy tremble of fear that raced through Lance's veins, came an unexpected flare of anticipation when she mentioned the famous matchmaker.

A mate? For him?

Yessssss.

"Lance, do you still have that cabin?" Elissa asked, eyes sparkling with mischief.

"Yeah, why?"

"I might need to borrow it for a few weeks."

"Of course, Nari."

Lance did not know why the Nari would be interested in the small vacation cabin he'd fixed up for himself a few miles out from the Pride House. The place had been nothing more than a shed when he'd bought it. After a year of working on it, he'd turned it into quite the little hideaway. But if Elissa wanted to borrow it, of course, she was welcomed to it.

He made a mental note to send her the code to the electric lock he'd put on the door. His Tiger was busy chuffing and scratching his long, thick claws against his skin from inside the metaphysical plane where the creature existed till called.

Mate.

His Tiger agreed the idea had merit. Maybe a visit from the infamous Uncle Uzzi was exactly what Lance needed.

Grrrrrrrr.

<h1 style="text-align:center">Chapter Two</h1>

"Hold the door, please."

The sound of a young woman's voice reached Uncle Uzzi's sensitive ears as he stood just inside the elevator of the upscale complex where he had recently bought a condo.

The young woman was breathing quite heavily, and she struggled with half a dozen shopping bags. Uncle Uzzi noticed she was trying to take a puff from an inhaler, and sympathy overwhelmed him. Uzzi rushed forward to take some of the burdens out of the woman's hands.

"Allow me, dear," he said, and the pretty stranger nodded, finally able to draw two quick puffs of much needed medicine into her lungs.

She held them in, eyes closed, while two tears rolled down her cheeks from the strain of trying to breathe. Uzzi waited, not pressing any buttons until the stranger could inhale and exhale normally again.

"Thank you so much. Darn asthma," the young woman replied. "Oh, that is better."

"My pleasure," Uncle Uzzi returned, noting the female's curly brown hair, equally dark eyes, and curvaceous figure.

She was just the type of woman his clients went wild for. Uzzi grinned, his magic zipping up and down his arms.

No wonder Hank called to say he was stuck in traffic.

The universe always had a plan, and it seemed Uncle Uzzi coming back to check on his little condo while he waited for his car was part of it. An idea began to take shape in his mind.

Perhaps he could be of some help to his new neighbor. He wondered what she would say when he broached the subject, but one look at one of her bags loaded with books from a local second-hand store, and he knew this would be easy peasy. The stranger was a fan of paranormal romance.

Fated indeed, he mused, and Uncle Uzzi smiled warmly.

"You're new in the building, aren't you, dear?"

"Me? Yes, *oh*, excuse me for not introducing myself," the young woman said, and blushed prettily. She reached out for her bags, and Uzzi detected an independent streak that was most attractive.

"Nonsense, you had all you could manage trying to get your breath back. It is quite fine."

"I am very sorry about that, and thank you for your help," she said, showing off white, straight teeth and a killer grin. "I am renting a unit for the season. My name is Annalia Reese."

"Nice to meet you. A temporary stay, then. I see. So, where are you from?" Uncle Uzzi said and returned her infectious smile with one of his own.

"I just got here from South Florida, actually."

"Ah. And how do you like it so far?" he asked, anxious to learn more about the intriguing young stranger.

Uzzi's magic was tingling, and his senses were on high alert. This one was special, whether she knew it or not. Uzzi had not run into Annalia Reese right then on accident. Fate had a hand in it. It always did.

"Well, I confess this weather is really something else. I don't think I was properly prepared," the woman shivered in her sneakers and lightweight coat.

Uncle Uzzi had to agree. She was not at all ready

for the kind of weather that was January in New Jersey. It was just after the New Year and the Garden State was a hodgepodge of snow, sleet, rain, and bitter winds.

"You poor thing," Uncle Uzzi said and nodded at her inhaler. "Asthma?"

"All my life," Annalia returned. "but this near attack was all my fault. I allowed myself to get in this shape."

"How do you mean?"

"Oh, not my body. I mean, I am a curvy girl, and all, but what I meant by allowing myself to get in this shape was that I ran out of my preventive medicine about a week ago. I knew I was traveling, but I forgot to refill it. I was working on a deadline and waiting on my prescriptions to be transferred here. It took a few days longer than I expected, but after some calls, I could finally pick it up a little while ago."

"Well, thank goodness for that, Annalia. My name is Uncle Uzzi," he told her and nodded his head. "How would you like to come to my place and warm up with a nice pot of tea, hmm?"

"Oh, that is so nice of you, but I wouldn't want to impose," she began.

"Not at all, I insist," Uncle Uzzi said, determined

to get to know the woman better.

His senses were rarely wrong, if ever, and Uzzi knew this young woman was going to be particularly important to someone in the immediate future. It was why he'd been pulled back to New Jersey when he'd had California in his sights.

Annalia didn't know it yet, but Uzzi was about to change her life. Trusting his instincts, he rattled off his condominium number and told her he would be expecting her as soon as she dropped off her things.

"Okay then, I'd love to. Just let me freshen up, and I will be right over," Annalia's friendly smile brightened her face, and Uncle Uzzi nodded at her.

"Of course," he said. It would give him just enough time to boil the water and muddle over his first impressions of her.

"I have a good feeling, liebling," he said to his late wife and walked into his condo.

The entire place was done in soft grays and stark whites. Clean, neat, and a little bit homey with the peach colored accents his decorator through in. Overall, Uzzi was quite happy with the finished space. He filled the kettle and set it to boil, preparing the teapot with some loose vanilla bourbon rooibos leaves.

Brewing tea was a ritual Uzzi often indulged in

when alone. He felt in tune with his powers whenever he did so, and it helped focus his magic, allowing him to trust his instincts.

This woman is important.

So important, he opened the box of pastries he'd brought up with him from the Bear Claw Bakery and began filling a dish with the delectable miniatures he'd purchased.

Food was also best when shared.

*A*n hour later...

"Uncle Uzzi, I have never had a cannoli cream filled chocolate dipped bear claw in my life but I swear this is the best thing I have ever eaten," Annalia sighed, placing her fork down on the plate.

The moist, fluffy dessert was simply scrumptious. But her favorite was the thick, dark chocolate fudge icing the bakery had dripped all over the buttery pastry. How they got it so light and fluffy was beyond Annalia, but dang, she definitely needed more of that in her life.

Her new neighbor was quite fascinating. Not only was he positively adorable with his snow white hair and beard, bright blue eyes, and charming grin, but he was also the owner of the world famous *Uncle Uzzi's Magical Matchmaking Service.*

"I am a devout fan of the Devlin brothers' confections," Uncle Uzzi agreed. "Do you cook?"

"Who me?" Annalia laughed and shook her head. "Afraid I can't boil water."

"I see," the older man chuckled his reply. "It isn't for everyone. What is it you do?"

"Oh, I am a graphic designer. I do a lot of freelance work for Graves Enterprises. I design and create avatars and fantasy landscapes for some of their video games."

"That sounds complicated," Uncle Uzzi remarked.

"The software can be a challenge at first since it is always changing. I recently started consulting with a company developing AI art software, and it is fascinating and a little frightening. These programs are creating art based on a string of text commands. The geeky side of me loves that it is a thing, but my artist's side is not really happy. Art is all about revealing the human soul. Artificial Intelligence is interesting, but it lacks emotion."

"I see," he murmured.

"Sorry, I get passionate about stuff like that.

When I create something, I just put so much of myself in the artistry," Annalia explained. She felt her cheeks heat with embarrassment.

"That is very interesting, but I know so little about graphic art."

"Oh, gosh, well, I know many people don't even think what I do is actual art. I know it's silly to get so worked up," she replied, shaking her head.

"Nonsense! Who told you that?" Uncle Uzzi snapped.

"Oh, it's not important."

"Of course it is! I have a nephew who creates video games, and I will have you know, I think they are just fantastic. They allow people from all walks of life to experience a world beyond their own reality or creative imaginings. You are an artist, Annalia. Don't let anyone tell you differently," the older man said firmly.

"Wow," she whispered. She could not put her finger on the reason, but sitting and chatting, sharing tea and snacks with the older man was perhaps the most relaxing thing she had done in a long while. Annalia could often lose herself in her work, and it was a solitary job, especially during the pandemic. She missed connecting with people on any level—this was nice.

"Thank you. I appreciate that."

"You sound surprised, dear," Uncle Uzzi replied, reaching for his tea. "Surely, you have friends or other family who feel the same?"

"Actually, I don't. I mean, I have a sister, but Sandra is a little bit out of the loop. She was married right out of high school, and her husband was very wealthy. They tied the knot the same year our parents died and took me in. She's never been a big fan of any kind of art."

"I am so sorry for your loss, child."

"Thanks, it's okay—I mean, it is never okay, but I am okay now. Better than I was, anyway. They were good people, died in an accident, and left us far too early. Dad had made some bad investments and Glenn pulled us out of the hole."

"Glenn is your sister's husband?"

"Yeah. He comes from old money, He's okay, I mean he was never bad to me, exactly. He is just weird about what he considers proper, and he hates my idea of art," she said blandly and sipped her vanilla infused tea.

Annalia sighed as the warm liquid soothed her throat and eased the ache inside her chest. Florida was all tropical heat no matter the month, and Jersey was super different. She'd come all this way, against her sisters' wishes, but it was important for her career.

Sandra was still mad at her and was giving her the silent treatment as punishment. She checked her phone, noting the same lack of reply to her daily text she sent to ask how her sister was doing.

Sigh.

"I don't want to sound like a complainer, I am grateful for them both. They paid for my college tuition, but I guess that's why they think they have the right to criticize."

"Family can be strange like that," Uncle Uzzi agreed.

"Totally. It's kind of why I made it a point to pay them back every cent they spent on tuition. In fact, I'll be finished this month. It would have been sooner, but I couldn't live with them another minute," she confessed.

Annalia smiled at the older man. This was so refreshing. She did not even stop to wonder why she could tell this kind stranger secrets she had not shared with anyone. It just felt so good to get it all out.

For the first time in a long while, Annalia had a friend.

Chapter Three

"Still, your sister must be very proud of you, being such a success," Uncle Uzzi remarked, handing her half of a strawberry jam infused bear claw.

Holy cow, I'm gonna gain a million pounds. But so worth it...

"You would think so, excuse me," Annalia replied, mouth full of deliciousness and swallowed before she continued with her explanation. "They don't approve of my job or the fact I refused to live with them. I think they just miss having a built-in babysitter for my nephew. He's a good kid, but my sister is his mother, and she needs to be the one raising him with his dad. Instead, they act like I abandoned them and always comment on how stupid I am to be paying rent when I could live with them instead."

Annalia shook her head, scoffing at the sheer gall of her sister and brother-in-law.

"That seems difficult. But you mentioned children, do you like them?"

"Oh, I love them. I just don't think it is my job to raise Sandra's son. I know when I have children, I want to be the one who takes care of them, me, and my husband—*if I ever get married*," she whispered the last, glancing down at her fingernails.

Annalia was a whiz with computers, but her love life left a lot to be desired.

Sigh.

"You know, so far, my dear, I have to tell you I think you are a smart, honest, and lovely woman. I do not understand your family's objections to your lifestyle. You seem hardworking and responsible."

"Awww, you are so sweet. Thank you," she whispered, feeling her cheeks grow warm. "I am so sorry for whining. It just feels so good to get this off my chest, I hope you don't think badly of me."

"Of course not, dear. And you aren't whining, it is perfectly natural to be frustrated with all you have been through. I would never judge you, my dear. We each have our own crosses to bear, but that doesn't mean we don't deserve a sympathetic ear now and then. Feel free to tell me anything, Annalia."

"I appreciate that," Annalia replied and flashed a small smile.

She hated feeling ungrateful, but her sister and family were such an energy suck. She really enjoyed sharing tea and pastries with the older man, even if she'd spilled her guts like he was some kind of therapist.

OMG. He is gonna think I am a total freak.

"Look, I should apologize for taking so much of your time. The tea and pastries were delicious, but I should probably go."

"Are you sure?"

"Oh, yeah. You must have things to do, but let me help clean up," she replied, taking her cup, saucer, and spoon, and walking it to the kitchen. She came back for the plate of pastries, just as Uzzi was standing.

"No, no, I got it," she told him, and he smiled and nodded as she took the rest of the dishes to the kitchen. Uzzi followed with the teapot.

"Thank you, my dear. You did not have to go through the trouble."

"My pleasure completely. I don't mind dishes, just don't ask me to do the laundry," she told him with a laugh.

"Deal," he said, smiling in return.

"Annalia, if you don't mind me asking, what about a boyfriend? Are you seeing someone right now?" Uncle Uzzi hedged.

"Seeing someone? Oh, no, I'm about as single as they come," she muttered.

"Is that by choice?'

"well, I guess, I mean, not really," she replied, loading the dishwasher. "I want to find a good man, but according to Sandra, I'll never be acceptable material for any man to seriously consider. Might as well not even try."

"Annalia, please forgive my frankness, but your sister is manipulating you, and it is affecting your self-esteem."

"You are probably right, but not everything she says is untrue. Just look at me. I dress for comfort, not style. I am allergic to most makeup. I get crazy ideas for work in the middle of the night and will spend hours at my desk without stopping until I have whatever I am working on just right. And I am a total nerd and will pick popcorn and Harry potter movies over a fancy dinner and night at the opera."

"You sweet child you, all I am hearing is that you are young, healthy, beautiful, smart, and honest. I know a dozen men who would cut off their right arms for a chance to date you." he stated, and Annalia snorted and shook her head.

"Yeah, right."

"I never joke about matters of the heart, dear. Incidentally, if you want a makeover, I can recommend a place where they cater to people with allergies like yours and use only the most gentle and natural ingredients, but only if you are interested," he informed her with emphasis.

"Organic makeup, huh? I admit, I am curious. You know, I'm an artist, but I have no ideas about style," she replied and dried her hands.

"Wonderful," Uncle Uzzi said, and waved his hand in the air. For a moment, Annalia thought she saw blue sparkles, but when she blinked, they were gone.

Odd.

"Let me find that card for you," Uzzi murmured, patting his pockets, and opening one drawer.

For the first time, Annalia considered whether she was interested in something like a makeover, or shopping in general. The truth was, she didn't like her sister's manipulations and criticism. Could that be why she hated looking for new clothes?

Yeah. Duh.

Sandra meant well, but she was forever putting Annalia down. Her sister was thin, blonde, and hardly ever had a hair out of place. She was Sandra's total opposite. Curvy body, curly, frizzy hair, dark eyes, and a big mouth. That was her.

Annalia could never capture attention like Sandra could from the opposite sex. Her sister was one of those neck-breakers, when she walked into the room, men's heads snapped to attention.

Sigh.

"Here we are," Uncle Uzzi said, handing her a card that read *Purrfect Products: Makeup so gentle even your cat will like it.*

Odd.

"And if you are interested in clothes, try this place," Uncle Uzzi handed her another card for *Jessica's Closet.* It seemed to be a boutique catering to women with fuller figures. That was exactly what Annalia needed. Awesome!

"Thanks. Ooh, they carry *Kisses by Kylie*, I hear that lingerie line is exquisite, but honestly, looking sexy isn't a concern these days."

"Dear, you are young and healthy, why on earth would that not be a concern?"

"Uncle Uzzi, my sex life is about as exciting as my wardrobe," Annalia replied and laughed out loud at her bad joke.

"I admit, I am surprised to hear that, Annalia. Can I ask you something?"

"Sure."

"If you aren't comfortable, you don't have to answer, but I am in the relationship business, so I'm naturally curious. Do you like sex?" the older man inquired, and Annalia was floored by the question.

"Like it? Sure, I mean, I *have* liked it. But to figure out what I like now, I would have to actually engage in some sex with another person," she replied honestly, cheeks heating up again.

"How long are we talking here since you had good sex?"

"Um, well, I'm not a virgin or anything, but the last time I got naked with a man was less than remarkable and it was a while ago."

"Seems to me you need a new perspective, dear," Uncle Uzzi said.

Awkward, she thought. Her eyes widened and Annalia tried to think of a way to stop this from getting worse.

"Oh, *um*, Uncle Uzzi, I think you are very nice and all—"

"No! I mean, I am flattered, but I don't mean *me*, child," he replied, and his blue eyes twinkled. "What I meant to say was, how about you let me set you up on a date?"

"What? Who? Me?"

"A date, and yes, you," Uncle Uzzi said, smiling widely. "Annalia, if you allow me, I promise I will find the perfect man for you."

"A perfect man for me? I don't think he exists," she began, but the idea was tempting.

Wouldn't it be wonderful to meet someone who was genuinely interested in her? To talk to a man who wanted to hear what she had to say?

And then, of course, there was the whole sex thing. She could hardly recall the last time she'd seen an actual penis.

Sigh.

Thank god for her top drawer. Without a few *top picks* adult toys purchased discreetly over the years, Annalia would never get her freak on. Hell, she wouldn't even know what an orgasm was.

"Dear, *he* exists, believe me."

"Then what would the perfect man want with me? Uncle Uzzi, I have no delusions about myself. I know I am cute, but in today's world, I'm also considered fat and weird, and I have a terrible time with new people. I'm shy."

"Nonsense," Uncle Uzzi growled. "You are a lovely woman. Now, tell me what you want in a man."

"How about someone who wants to be with me? Frizzy hair, sweatpants, belly rolls, big thighs, and all?"

"I don't think that will be a problem, but you may want to wear something other than sweats on your first date," he told her with a good-natured laugh. "What else?"

"How about someone who appreciates that I have an actual appetite for food? I mean, Uncle Uzzi, I like salad, but I am not a rabbit. I won't live on it. The last man I went out with tried to make me promise to go on a diet on the very first date."

"That man sounds like an ass," Uncle Uzzi's eyes glowed royal blue before he continued. "Annalia, I swear that will not happen. I will introduce you to big, gorgeous, growly men who adore women with real bodies. My clients love curves, and the man I introduce you to, will love yours."

"Really?"

"Yes," he returned. "This is the part where I think you should sit down, dear."

"Uh oh. IS this mystery man some sort of underground criminal or something?" she asked, only half kidding.

"No, not a criminal," Uzzi told her. "Do you believe in the supernatural?"

"Supernatural? What, is it a ghost or something?"

Again, she laughed, but the tiny hairs on her arms and the back of her neck were standing up. Annalia's pulse began to speed up, as Uncle Uzzi's gaze bore into hers.

"No ghosts, Annalia. I saw your bag with the books you like to read. Tell me, what do you know about Shifters?"

"Shifters? You mean like the romance genre?"

"No, I mean like Shifters," Uncle Uzzi replied steadily and smirked.

"Um, are you trying to tell me Shifters are real?" she whispered. "I mean, I saw some leaked footage once of a man turning into a Wolf in new York City, but I thought it was some sort of internet prank," she began, eyes wide. "But I work for Graves Enterprises, and one of the darker rumors floating around is the company is run by a Werewolf, so I think I know better."

"Well, Annalia, let me assure you, Shifters aren't a prank. They are very real, and I happen to know some who are looking for a woman just like you."

Disbelief, curiosity, and hope warred with each other for dominance inside of her, and Annalia licked her lips.

"A woman like me?" she bit her lip.

"Of course." Uncle Uzzi nodded. "Now, if you agree, I will set you up with a Shifter who will treat you like the treasure you are."

"Is it safe?" she asked, for some reason believing this ol man without question.

Shifters were real. They were really real. All her years of reading and online roleplaying in games like *WolfMoon* have finally paid off. Annalia was ready for a change in her life, and this felt like the right path for her. In fact, this felt huge.

"Always. When I introduce a client to a potential mate, I guarantee his or her safety. No one will mess with you while I am protecting you. That said, I think you should know, I have an impeccable reputation for finding mates."

"What do you mean by mates? Like friends?" Annalia asked.

"Oh no, a mate is more than a friend." Uncle Uzzi

leaned forward. "To a Shifter, there is no one or thing in the universe that compares to his or her *fated mate*. It's destiny. You see, Shifters are dual-natured. They share their essence with an animal spirit that they are then able to manifest in the physical realm. A Shifter knows his or her mate upon meeting them. It's instinct, intuition, or a combination of the two."

"So, a mate is like a girlfriend?"

"Still so much more than that, Annalia. A mate is the one person he will place above all others. She is essentially made for that Shifter. Please excuse my use of pronouns, but I think in your case you would be looking for a male."

"Yes," she replied, swallowed the lump in her throat. "Your pronouns are perfect."

"To a Shifter male, his mate is the most important thing in the world. She is his reason for living. If you mate a Shifter, you will be cherished, worshipped, loved, and did I mention the sex is incredible?"

"But what if I am not his mate?"

"Annalia, if you allow me to work with you, at the very least you will have a hot date with loads of sweaty, delicious sex. What do you have to lose?"

Holy shit.

Uncle Uzzi had her at *hot date*. The promise of sex was icing on the cake. Annalia looked straight into Uncle Uzzi's eyes and decided to take a leap of faith.

"I guess I don't have anything to lose, Uncle Uzzi," Annalia said. "Sign me up!"

Chapter Four

"Welcome to *Jessica's Closet*," a redhaired woman with an infectious smile came running at them once they entered the small boutique.

"Uncle Uzzi? OMG! Does Elissa know you are here?" The beautiful woman embraced Uncle Uzzi, tucking her hand in his elbow while they exchanged pleasantries.

"Of course she does. Do you think I'd invade Maverick Point without letting the Nari know?"

"Oh, it's hardly an invasion," Jessica replied and turned to Annalia. "Who's this? Are you a new client?"

"Well, sort of—"

"Yay! You are going to love Uncle Uzzi. He's like everyone's uncle, so easy to talk to and simply charming."

"Yes, he truly is. My name is Annalia Reese, but you can call me Anna or Lia, either is fine," she replied, offering her hand to the vivacious female.

"Miss Jessica, we are here for your expert advice. Anna here needs a fresh look, and she is interested in some of Gretchen's new line of makeup," Uncle Uzzi grinned wickedly.

"I see, well, let's get you booked for a complete makeover with Gretchen," she started, taking a glance at Anna's wildly frizzy curls.

"Though, honestly, I flove your hair. It is so wild," Jessica said and from her expression Annalia believed the woman.

"I'll see if Pam is free, she does wonders with curly hair."

"Um, just a trim—" Annalia called out, but Jess was already on the phone.

She closed her eyes, counted to three, and decided to go with it. What could be the harm in allowing herself to be pampered for a weekend? Even if the date was shit, she'd have a haircut and some cool new clothes. Even better, she'd made a friend or two.

"So, when is it?"

"What?" she asked, dropping the sheer red panties with matching thing she was holding up onto the floor.

Get a hold of yourself, Anna.

"When is the date, silly?" Jessica asked and laughed.

She smiled and bent down to retrieve the panty and bra set, adding it to a shopping bag she'd gone to get for Annalia. She did not know why she was so embarrassed. This was a clothing store and the last time she checked, underwear still fell under that category. Besides, it wasn't like she'd been caught doing something naughty.

"Oh, duh me," Annalia replied. "Eight o'clock tonight. But because of the long drive and the impending weather, Uncle Uzzi insisted I stay at a cabin for the whole weekend."

"Oooh, nice!"

It was nice to have a little winter getaway. A quiet cabin with a view of the thick pine forest sounded superb. And Uncle Uzzi had assured her that if the date did not work out, she was free to enjoy her stay in the picturesque wintry setting free of any further entanglements.

That sounded especially great to Annalia. After

making the move from Florida, she had not had the chance to relax or make friends. So far, everyone she met in Maverick Point was kind, and according to Uncle Uzzi, they were good people.

It was prettier here too. The city she'd moved too was flush of slush and winter mush, as she called the snowy dirt mixture. Busy New Jersey roads seemed doomed to dwell in the muck during snowy season.

Anna loved the look of the snow frosted trees and pretty forests on the drive down. It was exactly the kind of inspiration she needed for the new *Ice Battles* game's winter fantasy landscapes she was working on. Using specialized graphic design software to make real 3D snow, among other things was a lot more difficult than it seemed.

She could do with a little inspiration. Of course, Annalia was there for more than the scenery. She was there to go on a date with a Shifter. A real, live, honest to kisses Shifter! Goosebumps popped up all over her arms as she imagined what her date would be like.

Would he like her? Would he be kind? What if he wanted to, er, come home with her? Was Anna ready for that step?

Yes, please, her inner voice practically screamed.

Okay, so maybe her dry spell had been long

enough. She'd never been promiscuous, but she would not say no to sex. That was *if* she liked him, of course. And provided he liked her. She wasn't a slut or anything.

Sheesh. No kidding. I had three sexual partners in thirty years.

After an hour of trying on clothes, she was finally ready for her hair appointment. Anna sighed and bit her lip. Her credit card was going to cry if she used it again, but only one more stop, she promised the little piece of plastic.

Truthfully, shopping had been fun—*especially without Sandra*. Guiltily, she pulled out her phone and checked to see if her sister read the message, she had sent the night before telling her she would be out of pocket for the weekend. It had been seen, but there was no reply. Of course not.

Ugh. Oh well.

Annalia was not going to play this game with her older sibling anymore. If Sandra wanted a relationship with her, she would have to grow up and work on one with her. Not leave it up to Anna to run after her like a little lost puppy.

Speaking of, she thought with a smirk and chased after Uncle Uzzi as he walked to the salon next door. Her arms were filled with bags, having bought everything from new underwear and body cream to a stylish winter coat, strappy high heels, and a pair of sturdy boots.

"Hello Pam! How is *osito*?" Uncle Uzzi greeted a pretty brunette with a hug and a smile before turning to Annalia. "You are in good hands, Annalia. Pam is the best. Now, I have an errand to run, but I will be back to collect you soon," Uncle Uzzi told her and said goodbye.

She had one moment's hesitation before sitting in the salon chair the woman indicated.

"Hi Annalia, I'm Pamela," the very lovely, very pregnant brunette introduced herself with a kind smile as she started running her hands through Anna's hair. "Let's see what we got to work with. So, how long have you known our Uncle Uzzi?"

"Hi Pam, my name's Annalia. We just met, but he's great," she smiled.

"Anna-Leah? Am I saying that right?"

"Yes, but it is spelled A-n-n-a-l-i-a," she told her.

"Great name! I am making a list since my husband and I, and our son Paulie, can't seem to agree on one for this little bundle," she replied and nodded at her protruding belly.

"Congrats, is it a girl?"

"We don't know yet. Twins," she practically yelped.

"That is exciting. Say, can I ask you a question?"

"Sure."

"Is everyone here beautiful?

"Ha ha ha! You're funny." Pamela laughed, ignoring her question. "*Hmm.* Your hair is good, but I think you could use a trim and a conditioning treatment."

"Can you blow it out? I kind of have a date tonight," she bit her lip again.

"Absolutely. Did Uncle Uzzi set you up?"

"Yep."

"Well, then, we better get to work. This could be a life-changing event," Pamela said.

The woman must be teasing her, but butterflies began to build inside her stomach. Pam was kind and friendly. Settling into the salon chair, closing her eyes as the stylist worked her magic, she allowed herself to float.

The buzzing of her cell phone caught her attention, and when Pam excused herself for a potty break, Annalia grabbed the thing. It was Sandra. Looked like her big sis had finally deigned to reply. Probably the thought of Annalia going on a weekend retreat bugged the shit out of her, but wait, that was not kind. The least she could do was open the text messages.

I can't believe you went all the way to Jersey, Annie. Don't you think it's time you stopped being selfish? Glenn Jr. has gold practice in the afternoons and no one to take him. There are papers needing signatures and the work you left behind is really piling up. How irresponsible can one person be?

Now, if you are ready to stop this ridiculous tantrum, I can find my way back to forgiving you and let you come home again. But this offer is not open ended, Annie. You owe me and Glenn.

-Sandra

Annalia blinked back the tears that burned her eyes. Her sister was always doing things like that. She'd been making her sign these papers for years concerning Glenn's business and them being her guardians, and the loan papers for school.

The last packet she'd signed before leaving had been super long and complicated. Annalia hadn't even had a chance to look it over. But she trusted Sandra, and now that she was finished with graduate school and running her own business, Anna had one more payment to make before they were paid back in full. Glenn had insisted she sign the last round of papers before she moved to New

Jersey, and she'd done it to keep them all on friendly terms.

But calling her by that godawful nickname, *Annie*, and saying she was selfish were the last straw. One payment left, then she wouldn't owe them a thing. Shaking her head, Anna dropped the phone back into her purse. She was going to studiously ignore her condescending big sister until then.

All she wanted to do was work on her graphic designs and be happy. Why did Sandra always have to try to make her feel guilty for that? She was thirty-years old. Not a child anymore. She wanted her own life, and her own chance to find happiness. What was wrong with that?

"Nothing at all, honey," Pamela replied sympathetically, and Annalia blushed. She'd spoken aloud.

Shit on a shingle.

She really hated to air her dirty laundry, but she supposed that was a side effect of hair salons.

"You know it is. We're like therapists, but better because we make you look good too," Pamela went on.

Dang it. Anna realized she'd spoken aloud again. The beautiful woman winked before continuing in an easy going manner that put Annalia immediately at ease.

"Look, your big sister means well, I'm sure, but we all have a right to happiness and love. Now, you take it from someone who owes her own happiness to Uncle Uzzi, you are in excellent hands."

"I sure hope so."

"I know so," she answered. "Now, what do you think?"

Pamela spun the salon chair around, and Anna gasped. Her mass of wild brown curls was completely transformed into a glossy, sleek blow-out that curled around the ends like a 1950s glam girl.

"Oh damn, is that really me?"

The look emphasized her big, brown eyes, bringing attention to her full lips and high cheekbones. Her face was a little round, but she was a bigger girl. Her Italian heritage shown in her straight nose and olive-tone skin.

"Yes, it is you." Pamela smiled and patted her belly.

"Hey guuuurrrrrrllllllll!" Marion, another stylist, came running over and high-fived his co-worker. "She's got you looking fine as hell! Way to go, Pam!"

"Thanks, Marion. I used that gloss you suggested."

"Well, that's fine and good. But you know Miss

Annalia here came in with those gorgeous locks, honey. You just made 'em shine."

"Truth," Pam agreed.

"Thank you, both. I love it."

Annalia was all smiles as she left with her bags and new hairstyle. Uncle Uzzi sent the car back for her, complete with his hunky driver. He'd introduced himself as Hank and placed her bags in the trunk.

Anna was a little shy of him. He was big and strong. A Shifter according to Uncle Uzzi, but she was still a little wary of the whole idea that the supernatural existed.

Even the old matchmaker confessed he was not entirely human. He was, in his words, a Witch descended from the goddess of love, herself. Annalia was just blown away. Still, every instinct told her to trust these people, so she did.

Smiling to herself, she enjoyed the quiet ride to the rental cabin. It was short and pretty. The entire town of Maverick Point, even the beautiful mountain in the background, seemed to have been bathed in a blanket of snow and ice. Like the scene inside a snow globe. She hardly noticed the car had stopped when Hank held her door open.

"Miss?"

"Oh, thank you," she said and allowed him to help her from the vehicle.

Hank carried her bags to the porch, and she waved goodbye. Annalia had just enough time to rest and take her inhaler before she got dressed. She felt exhilarated and anxious all at the same time. Maybe not anxious, maybe it was just anticipation at tonight's date.

Who knew shopping could be so much fun? Certainly, it never was in her experience. Then again, Sandra had always been there to let her know what a woman with her figure should and should not wear.

Sigh.

Well, if her sister could see the racy, sexy, and surprisingly comfortable choices she'd made, she would probably drop dead on sight.

Ouch. That was mean.

Anna bit her lip as mixed feelings filled her. She was sure Sandra loved her—in her own messed up way. Still, leaving Florida and getting away from the nagging negativity that was her sister was the best thing she'd ever done for herself.

She'd taken a leap of faith today and trusted a total stranger about things she'd only ever read about in those naughty little romance books she was addicted to.

But for the first time, Annalia felt excited about something other than work. She was finally going for the things she wanted out of life, and yes, it was scary as fuck, but that would not stop her. Uncle Uzzi was right.

Here we go. Time to start living.

Chapter Five

A few hours earlier...

"Lance Jacosa! Doesn't look like you changed at all since I was last here, despite Elissa telling me you were wasting away for want of a meeting."

That voice! Those twinkling blue eyes. It was him. The one man in the world, save his Neta, who made Lance quake with nervousness.

Fuck.

He walked over cautiously—*like any predator worth his salt would when about to engage with someone of equal, or perhaps greater, power*—to greet the older male Witch.

Energy buzzed around the man in the form of tiny blue sparks. Lance's Tiger approved of his aura, seemed impressed by the wealth of magic the male seemed to have at his disposal. It was undeniable. Uncle Uzzi's magnetic pull was damn near impossible to resist.

Dammit.

He had been hoping to go unnoticed. Admitting he had cold feet was embarrassing as fuck for a male in Lance's position. Still, he could not help but feel wary. What could he possibly have to offer a mate?

"Let's see," the old Witch said with a discerning eye, gaze raking over Lance like hot coals. "You still have that handsome face the ladies can't resist, I see."

Lance froze in place and turned to greet the man he'd been equally dreading and anticipating over the last week. Clad in a brilliant white coat with a red scarf wrapped around his neck, Uncle Uzzi gazed at him for a good, long minute. The older Witch's blue eyes flashed with magic as he sized the Tiger up.

He was more magician than matchmaker. A Witch with some sort of connection to a love goddess or some crap like that—at least, that was what the rest of the Pride said about the guy.

Truly, he had the entire supernatural world in awe of his phenomenal matchmaking skills. He found mates for Shifters who were the worst of the worst. Lance was not all that bad. He just had a sort of a reputation, and, *er*, his Tiger was getting kind of angsty.

"Uncle Uzzi," Lance replied, thinking of ways to talk his way out of this whole thing.

It was obvious to Lance he'd made a mistake. He was much too young to get mated. Maybe he just needed a vacation. When Elissa and Jessica had cornered him the other day, he never expected them to actually call the matchmaker.

Grrrrrrr.

His Tiger dug his claws in, and Lance stayed rooted to the spot. Fucking hell. What did a guy have to do to keep his bachelorhood safe around here? Lance was supposed to be the fun guy, the good uncle, a no strings fuck buddy. He was not a happy-ever-after kinda Cat.

Rrrrroooaaaaaaaaaaaarrrrrrrrrrr.

Alright already, I'll hear the man out, he growled back at his inner beast.

His Tiger chuffed angrily, refusing to remove his claws from inside his gut. The Cat was beyond grouchy. No wonder. The ornery animal hadn't allowed Lance to have sex in months. No surprise Jessica and the Nari had heard all those rumors about him. Lance's rep was in the dirt and all because of his beast.

Fuck our reputation, the Tiger snarled.

Lance grimaced and cleared his throat. It was time he faced facts. The animal wanted a mate.

"No use trying to run from your pussy cat, Lance my boy. The beast wants a mate. Shall we chat?"

"Yes, *er*, please," he grumbled in reply.

What else could he do? He'd already rented out his cabin to the woman. Lance had been sleeping in the Pride House the last few weeks anyway. His Tiger needed the company.

Though solitary animals in the wild, Tiger Shifters were different. Communal groups helped them control their natural inclinations to animalistic behavior. The fact his Tiger was becoming increasingly aggressive and unruly was worrisome, but predictable. This kind of thing happened sometimes when a Shifter remained unmated.

His beast was built to protect and guard. The problem was he had nothing of his own to keep safe. Startling as it was, Lance understood he needed that. Needed a mate, a cub, a family—not just a Pride. He needed something to anchor him, to concentrate on, and to, *gulp*, love.

Fuck, was he really doing this?

Yessss, his Tiger hissed.

"I see you," Uzzi whispered, seeming to talk right to his animal, and the Tiger roared his reply.

"Uncle Uzzi, I know you are here to help, but I am doing just fine—"

"Fine is it," the older man removed his coat and took the seat across from him, "Word is you've lost a step."

Grrrr.

"Easy," he said, raising one eyebrow at him before continuing. "The fact is I can help you. If you do not believe me, then simply listen. Lance, your Tiger is trying to tell you something."

"Like what?" he snarled the question.

"Like those women you've been spending time with aren't for you," Uncle Uzzi insisted.

He placed his hands palms down on the table and closed his eyes. The Tiger inside him chuffed, nudging him, encouraging him to listen.

Fuck.

As a member of the Neta's Guard, Lance needed to regain control, sooner rather than later. Pride's had different ways of dealing with members who proved too unpredictable, and Lance was terrified he would endanger those he'd sworn to protect if this went on too long.

Everyone was right. He needed a mate.

"You are right. But, Uncle Uzzi, where am I going to find *her?*"

"Leave that to me, but first, I have a question."

"Shoot."

"Do you have a suit?"

Hours later...

"I feel like an asshole," grumbled Lance.

"Well, you look like *Prince Charming*. Stop that," Elissa stomped over and took the tie from his hands. "Here now. Hunter?"

"What happened? Elissa, are you okay?" The Neta came running into the room, skidding to a stop in front of his mate. His hands ran over her shoulders and waist, but the Nari growled, and slapped at him.

"Stop it, honey. Now, look at Lance," she instructed, and the man looked confused. "Doesn't he look nice?"

"What?" he growled.

"I mean it. He's wearing a suit, all dressed up like a stud. Doesn't he look sexy? *Ooof!*" Elissa's breath left her lungs as the Neta swung her into his arms.

"Mine," the Neta snarled, and Lance about crapped himself. Was she trying to get him killed?

"Fuck, yes, she is yours, Neta," he growled, the amount of Alpha power in the room damn near suffocating him.

"Hunter! Stop it," she replied, all giggles for her mate.

"Neta?" Lance gasped, almost going to his knees.

"Shit. Sorry, Lance," Hunter growled and relented. He stared down at his mate.

"Woman, you had me thinking something happened to you," he grumbled.

"Nothing happened to me, silly Tiger. I'm fine."

The Neta growled and caught her lips in a rough kiss that Lance could not help but watch. Their love story was legend, and for a moment, he had the tiniest spark of hope that maybe, just maybe, he could have the same—if Uncle Uzzi came through for him.

But what if he fucked it up? What if she hated him?

Fuck. Please don't let me be an asshole. Let her like me a little. Shit.

He did not even know who she was, but Lance was already sending wishes out into the universe. Praying for someone to love him like Elissa loved Hunter.

"Now, what did you say about him looking sexy? I'll show you sexy," Hunter grumbled and smacked her on the ass, which elicited a response Lance would rather die than witness.

"Hunter," Elissa growled, but her eyes swung back to Lance a second longer before lust could take over the ruling couple. "Lance, make sure you are on your best behavior. And compliment her. No sex until you talk to her!"

The Neta spanked his mate again, dragging another moan from her lips, before he carted her off to their bedroom. Lance shivered.

Blech.

It was like listening to your parents make out —*what could be worse?*

Actually catching them doing it. Which he almost had just the other day. Thank fuck for his supernaturally enhanced Tiger hearing. Brayden had already shared a horrifying story of catching the two of them going at it that damn near scarred Lance. The poor Beta couldn't look at either Neta or Nari for a week afterwards.

Ewww.

"Why me?" Lance whispered and rolled his eyes.

He checked his watch. It was half an hour until he had to pick up his mystery date, and the cabin was about fifteen minutes away. He should wait a little bit, but the sounds of moaning coming from the next room made up his mind for him.

"Hell no," he muttered.

Sighing, Lance grabbed the keys to his custom Range Rover P525 and headed out the door in his suit and tie. The SUV had a black leather interior with soft, orange LED lights on the floors. It reminded him of his Tiger, so he'd bought the thing on sight.

Money was something he did not have to worry about anymore. Lance worked for *Maverick Development* on Brayden's crew, but that was more for the physical release and sense of companionship than a necessity.

He'd invested his money wisely and had a nice little nest egg he was sitting on. He also did a lot of paperwork for the Pride as well. Keeping things like their licenses, birth certificates, and stuff like that from looking suspect to humans.

Shifters aged differently, and some had extended lifespans. Still, it was important to blend in to keep the Shifter secret. History had taught them how humans as a whole reacted to proof of the supernatural—*witch trials, mass hysteria, war, genocide*—and it was decided long ago by people smarter than him that it was better for everyone this way.

Lance did his part for the Pride to keep them safe from detection. Whether he worked outdoors with the crew, or online in the office, he did his part for the community. There was nothing like putting in a day's work to make a man feel good.

Hence the log cabin project. He'd bought the parcel of land from the Pride, approving of the way it felt secluded but wasn't. Not really. The town and Pride House were less than twenty minutes away. He'd made sure to add all the modern amenities necessary to be comfortable.

Electricity, plumbing, gas.

The ten surrounding acres were secluded woods that allowed him to Shift and roam in his fur. It was ideal, but lonely. He needed someone to share it with. It had been sitting there, empty for weeks.

Elissa had only just confessed that when she'd asked for the key code, it was for to Uncle Uzzi. At the time, he didn't know his blind date would be staying there. Nerves assailed him. What if she hated it?

Fucking hell.

Snow was falling more rapidly, and the wind was blowing hard as he exited the vehicle and bounded up the stairs to rap on the door.

"One minute," a voice called from inside, and Lance felt his entire body tense.

His Tiger pushed forward, leaving his chest muscles straining against the silk shirt he had on.

Lance hated getting dressed up, but Uncle Uzzi had arranged for their first date to be the *Winter Wonderland Wine & Tapas Charity Ball.*

The tickets were five-thousand dollars a person. All proceeds went to benefit an environmental organization working on preserving the Pine Barrens. Something which, as a Shifter, he felt very strongly about.

Tickets purchased, suit on, he'd headed out with the intention of enjoying a mundane night out. Only now, his entire being seemed on high alert. As he listened to the lock on the door turn, Lance sucked in a deep breath.

Holy fuck.

That did not work out as intended. He'd thought to calm himself, but the delicious scent he'd sucked in only whet his appetite further.

The most intoxicating fragrance he'd ever smelled wrapped around his senses. Like a soft, warm hand brushing across his arms, chest, belly, all the way down to his suddenly rock-hard cock.

Chocolate and cherries, laced with chili peppers--the good kind that left a long, slow, honest sizzle after the sweet was gone.

Well, that's one question answered.

Lance sniffed again and adjusted his too-tight

pants. His Tiger roared in his head. The heavenly-scented female was pulling the door open, but time slowed as she did. Inch by inch, it felt like forever until, *finally*, he saw her.

The entire world fell away in the moment she was revealed, and Lance damn near swallowed his tongue. The woman was gorgeous. Soft curves perfectly outlined in a crimson velvet dress that enhanced the olive tone of her skin and the deep, chestnut hues in her hair.

Eyes the color of chocolate—*the expensive kind with eighty percent cacao*—flashed at him from under long, curled lashes. Her bottom lip was plump and juicy, and fuck, he wanted to spend days just nibbling on it. She had the cutest little dimple on her chin, and her breath seemed to catch as she glanced over him from head to toe.

Lance was already a goner, but her perusal had him freezing in place. He hoped she found him alright.

Mine.

Chapter Six

"**M**ine."

Fuck.

He'd whispered that aloud. Thank the gods for the small gust of wind that came, whisking his words away before the beautiful normal could hear them. He breathed deep, sucking in her flavors once more.

Yes, the female was human. But if she knew Uncle Uzzi, she knew about Shifters. Still, knowing was different from *knowing*. He did not want to scare her off with his growling.

Cool it, he told his beast. Fucking Cat was too damn eager.

"Hi," she said, smiling brightly. "I'm Annalia

Reese. You can call me Anna, though. I hope you don't mind that Uncle Uzzi set this up."

Her smile wobbled a little as she waited for him to say something, but he couldn't talk. Not just yet. She cleared her throat and left him to follow her in or stay in the doorway. He stood there. Like an idiot.

Annalia. Pretty name for a pretty girl.

"I just need my coat. Oh, I'm sorry, you said something when I opened the door, but I couldn't hear you. The wind was blowing," she explained.

"Oh, uh," he muttered.

I'm a fucking idiot.

Lance opened and closed his mouth a few times like a moron. But what could he do? It was *her*. She was *the one*. His fated mate. He was certain.

This woman was his destiny. Every instinct screamed at him to cart her off to the bedroom and claim her. He wanted to desperately.

The urge was so strong it almost brought him to his knees. Lance wanted to make love to her in a thousand and one ways. To kiss her, fuck her, bite her, and claim her. To mark her with his scent, his cum, his teeth. To make sure she bore his mark.

Yes. Mine. Do all that. Get her swollen with our cubs.

Shut up, idiot monster.

He was trembling with the strength it took to rein in his Tiger. He just had to remember she was human. The need to fuck and bite and claim were not going to be instant for her. She needed patience and wooing.

Want her. Now. Lick. Kiss. Bite. Claim.

How about I tell her my name first, idiot.

"Oh, um, I'm Lance," he replied, voice cracking.

Fuck, that was embarrassing. He cleared his throat and tried again.

"Um, sorry. I'm Lance Jacosa and I am definitely glad Uncle Uzzi set this up. I hope you are okay with it?"

"Sure, otherwise I wouldn't be here. No harm in a date, right?" she asked, and shrugged nonchalantly, but he could hear her heart pounding.

Her breath was raspy, and she looked a little pale. Lance frowned and stepped forward. Was she hurt? He managed to control himself as she turned around, as if searching for something.

Ah, her bag.

She lifted the small black clutch and smiled, doing a little victory shimmy, and grabbing her coat with her other hand.

"Found it," she murmured and blushed prettily.

"Are you ready?"

He grinned at her. How could he not? She was adorable.

"Yes, thank you."

Annalia smiled and took his proffered arm. The feel of her small hand in the crook of his elbow made his pulse race, and his beast perk up. The Tiger liked her hands on him.

Suddenly, his whole world had shifted. Annalia was beautiful and her scent was intoxicating. But Lance knew he needed to take it slow. She was human and would not understand his certainty that she was the one for him. Patience was not exactly his strong suit, but for her, he could learn. She was already more than he had ever hoped for.

Once situated in the car, Lance turned the seat warmer on her side. He needed to be mindful of her delicate human nature. She was fragile, meant to be cherished.

Fuck, how he wanted to cherish her—*with every single inch of him.*

"So, I know this is crazy, and maybe I am being too forward, but well, I met Uncle Uzzi in the building where I am renting a condo and he told me he's like this dating expert. He also noticed my preferred reading material, and well, he told me some things that might be a little, *er,* crazy."

"Crazy how?"

"Well, I don't really know why he told me the things he did—"

"What did he tell you?"

"He said magic was real, and supernatural stuff, too. I guess what I want to know is, was he telling the truth? Are you a Shifter?" she asked in a whisper.

He could feel her embarrassment and his beast did not like that. She should feel comfortable enough to ask him anything. Biting back his growl at the thought he did anything to make her uncomfortable, Lance answered her questions as best he could.

"Uncle Uzzi has his reasons, and I am not privy to them. But Annalia, I swear I will always tell you the truth. I am a Shifter. Does that bother you?"

Lance could not stop the pounding of his heart. He could not believe how much her answer mattered to him, but it did. Her comfort and safety were paramount to anything he might be feeling, and Lance would do his best to soothe any fears she might have about his Cat.

"Oh, wow. So, you are? Shifters are real," she muttered, more to herself than to him.

Lance stayed silent, waiting for her to process the information. Eyes on the road, he listened to her breathing. Raspy again, and he frowned.

"Uh, what kind of Shifter are you?"

The scent of her nervousness had his Cat yowling mournfully, but he reined in the beast. She was a human. This was new for her.

Go slowly. Don't fuck it up.

As far as pep talks went, it was the best he had. Lance sucked in a breath, savoring that spicy chocolatey scent that was all Annalia.

Anna, she'd said to call her, but he liked her whole name. It was unique, just like her. She was so perfect, but fear and lies did not belong between them. So, he decided to just straight shoot it.

"I'm a Bengal Tiger Shifter," he explained. "I can Shift into my animal at will, and though we share our existence, he has his own personality quirks."

"Wow," she answered, a smile splitting her face. It was like the sun coming out, seeing her grin so widely, and Lance knew he wanted to make her smile as often as possible.

"I love tigers. They're my favorite animal. So, what are some of his quirks?"

"Well," he replied, clearing his throat. It got all growly when she said she loved tigers. His beast was practically strutting now.

"It's not a quirk per se, but right now my Tiger is thinking you smell fantastic."

"Oh," she replied, lips forming a perfect circle.

That mouth of hers was so fucking hot. Gonna get them both in trouble if he didn't keep imagining it wrapped around his cock. He squirmed in his seat. Damn this fucking suit.

The slim fit pants Elissa had insisted on were cutting off the circulation to his balls. Or maybe that was because his entire blood supply was currently in his dick.

"I am glad he likes how I smell," she told him, and damn, he was definitely gonna throw this fucking suit out after tonight.

"I like it very much," he told her, loving the way she seemed to glow under the small praise

Compliment her often. Check.

His sweet mate had the cutest little smile, bringing her dimple out, practically begging him to trace it with his tongue. Lance was already imagining what it would feel like to be able to kiss and nibble on her whenever he wanted.

Slow. Go slow.

Grrrr.

Yep. It was going to be a long night. He caught her watching him watch her and he tried to relax. He didn't want to frighten her with the strength of his desire, but fucking hell, that was going to be hard.

Hard.

Yes, hard. For her.

Oh, that was great. Now, he was thinking about his dick again.

Change the subject, growled his Cat.

"Like music?"

"Sure," she agreed.

"What kind?"

"Anything is fine," she said.

"I insist, you pick," he told her and nodded to the dashboard.

"Okay, but I am warning you, I don't play around."

"What does that mean?" he asked, liking her spunk.

"It means I am not going to tune into something I think you'll like. If you are telling me to pick something I like, then I am really going to choose what I want to hear."

"Good," he said and meant it. "I want to know what music you like, Annalia. I'm curious about you."

"Really?"

She blinked slowly, her soulful brown eyes ever watchful before she turned her attention to the satellite radio.

"Yeah, really. I know it is soon for you, but I like you, Annalia."

"You like me? Oh. Um, okay. Well, then, this is our first compatibility test."

Lance laughed as she tuned into a retro eighties station. The *Go-Go's* were going on vacation, and why the heck not? He winked at her, then started singing along in his deep baritone. The beautiful woman laughed aloud, relaxing visibly beside him.

Good, he thought.

His Tiger chuffed softly inside his chest, the noise mimicking a purr. Shock and then absolute pleasure rolled through him when she joined him in singing.

Fuck, she was so cute.

Her voice was delightfully off key, but it was music to his ears. The trip to the event was over far too quickly. He pulled up to the valet attendant, a smile on his face, looking forward to the ball.

Elissa and Jessica had been right. Uncle Uzzi had found her. This woman was it for him. His destiny. His mate.

Mine.

Now, he just had to win her heart.

Chapter Seven

Oh my.

Anna licked her lips, casting a side-long glance at the huge, handsome man on her arm. She was going to have to send Uncle Uzzi a gift basket or something.

Even if this lasted just the one night, her date was the most gorgeous man she'd ever seen. Tall and wide, with short, tawny-colored hair, and a grin that made her panties melt clean off her body.

He was sex personified. A veritable magnetic force in his own right, drawing stares from passing women as they waited their turn in the check in line. She waited for the green-eyed monster to show up, but all she could muster was pride.

Anna was proud to be the woman on his arm,

and she relished having all his smexy attention just for herself. Lance was courteous and so much fun. And even better—he only had eyes for her. Imagine that?

When he started singing along with the eighties station she put on, she couldn't help but laugh. He had good taste in music, too. Damn, he was perfect.

In Anna's experience, men who looked like that did not pay attention to girls like her. But he seemed to like her more than that too. In fact, the heat in his sapphire gaze was mesmerizing.

"Did I mention how gorgeous you look?" he asked as he stood, holding their coats while they waited to hand them to the young woman working the check-in.

They stood among a large throng of people, but Lance's eyes hadn't left her, not once. Especially not since she took off her long coat. Anna bit her lip nervously. The deep red dress was made of the softest material she'd ever felt. There had to be some sort of elastic sewn within it because it molded to her curves like a second skin, leaving very little to the imagination. Though technically, she was fully covered.

The strapless confection made her feel like a character in a fairytale. She'd been nervous about it at first, but Jessica had insisted she looked amazing. Between the hair and the dress, and the sexy bustier and thong set she'd picked up in the boutique, Anna had to admit she felt great.

That little bit of naughty lace gave her the extra boost of confidence she needed to pull off the whole ensemble. Uncle Uzzi had been right. Sometimes dressing sexy was good for the soul.

She was trying the new allergen free makeup she purchased, but even then, she only wore some face powder, a tiny bit of mascara, and some red tinted lip gloss. The products were new to her, and Anna would rather not spend half the night in the bathroom trying to keep her eyes from tearing like they always did in reaction to cosmetics.

She'd been nervous at first, but with the way Lance was watching her, Anna felt pretty. Every now and then, she saw a gold glint in his eyes.

"You bring out the Tiger," he'd whispered in her ear when she had asked him about it.

The idea of his Tiger thrilled Anna. She wanted to ask him to show her but didn't know if that was against any Shifter rules or anything. Hell, it might just be bad manners. This was only their first date. With time, maybe she would get to see his beast. If he wanted to see her again, of course.

She frowned, wondering if this was a once off, but then the pressure of his large hand on her waist nudged her forward, and she snapped back to the present. Shivers raced down her spine at the platonic touch. Was it normal for a woman to be so worked up over a man she had only just met?

Hardly an expert on the subject, Anna knew one thing for certain. Ever since she'd opened the cabin door and saw the huge, sexy man standing there, she hadn't been able to breathe quite right, and it had nothing at all to do with her asthma.

"This is taking long," he murmured and peered ahead. "My apologies. I had no idea, or I'd have taken you to our seat first."

Oh, wow.

Anna wasn't even listening to what he was saying, she was so awestruck by his profile. He was like model gorgeous. And even better, he seemed completely unaware. She loved his deep-set eyes, straight nose, and that perfectly chiseled chin. His cheekbones were defined, but not overly so. Really, it was that smattering of five o'clock shadow that covered his jawline that did it for her.

It gave his positively beautiful face a sexy and rugged edge. She was dying to run her fingers through it, to feel his hair-roughened cheek against her skin. Especially that spot right between the cleft in his chin, where it appeared just a touch thicker.

Damn, is it hot in here?

If he kept this up, she was going to need a fan. And new panties. Of course, it wasn't just his face. The rest of him was damn fine looking, too. He had one of those V-type bodies. Wide shoulders tapering into a narrow waist that blended to long, muscular legs.

If she could've gone through a catalog of male parts, she wouldn't have been able to come up with anything as perfect as he was physically. But damn, she'd have fun trying. Uncle Uzzi was right. Shifters were hot. With any luck, he'd be hot for her by the end of the night.

Down girl. Your slut-o-meter is ringing off the charts.

Oh well. A girl could dream, couldn't she?

"Are you okay? Waiting, I mean."

He cocked his head to the side and looked at her with his blue eyes glowing a tad in the dimly lit hallway.

"I'm fine," she replied easily. "I don't mind waiting."

Of course, she didn't. Not when she could spend that time with him. The small talk they'd made in the car was fine, but not informative. And here she was sizing him up like some prize pony at the state fair. She was almost ashamed of herself, but really. How was she supposed to react? She'd never had a date who looked like him. He grinned and winked at her, the wicked smile telling her he knew exactly what she was thinking.

Crap.

Anna was like one giant hormone around him. Her ovaries were working double time just thinking about the muscles she spied beneath that outrageously sexy suit he wore. She should ask him some questions. Especially, if she was already thinking about getting naked with him.

"So, what do you do for a living?" she cleared her throat, attempting a conversation.

Lance quirked his head and grinned. She could see he was surprised by the question. Well, good. She'd just have to keep on surprising him.

"I work for Maverick Development, on a construction crew. I also take care of the Pride's paperwork, and I do some computer stuff as well."

"Really? Like what?"

"Uh, I dabble in programming. Firewall installation. I used *Draco Fortis* products for most of our security needs. And, I have some investments," he muttered and ducked his head.

It was as if he was embarrassed. A ruddy color spread across his face, and she gasped. OMG. He was blushing. Laughter bubbled up inside of her, and she poked him in the ribs playfully.

"What are you? Some rich boy playing at construction or something?" she teased.

He did drive a nice vehicle. The suit he wore was obviously tailored to his magnificent build. But he was so down to earth, it was difficult to reconcile.

"I'm not rich, rich, but I have invested wisely. Is money important to you?" he asked.

"Not really," she shrugged and looked straight.

The couple in front of them was taking forever to get situated. Anna was a straight shooter, so she figured now was as good a time as any to tell him about her family.

"I was in my teens when my parents died, and my sister and her husband raised me. His family is loaded so money is very important to them. But the truth is, I never felt like their money made them happy. I mean, I'm not stupid. It is good to have money, but it isn't everything."

"I agree," he told her, running a finger down her arm and bringing forth delicious little shivers. "Money is nice. Security is nice. But there are other things that matter more."

"Exactly. As for me, I work hard and I love my job, I do graphics work mostly for Graves Enterprises. It's why I came up here from Florida, to be closer to their main offices. I make a decent living."

"Wow, you're an artist? That's awesome," he said, his smile heart-stopping and her heart thudded heavily.

Careful, Annalia. You're gonna fall hard.

"I mean, technically yes, I create art using software, but I'm not like Monet or something," she replied, her embarrassment making her cheeks burn.

"That's some bullshit there. Listen, Anna, you put your heart and soul in what you do, that makes you an artist. You own that and be proud of it. Anyone who tells you otherwise is just trying to manipulate you, and they aren't worth your time."

His eyes flashed gold when he talked, and his voice was all deep and growly. Anna stared and nodded. He was right, of course. Glenn and Sandra were the two biggest manipulators she knew.

"You hit the nail right on the head," she told him.

"I am guessing it's your sister and husband who told you those lies about your work. Can I ask, what does your brother-in-law do?"

"Oh, I don't know. He's always really vague. Glenn has investments, like you, I guess," she said and shrugged as they moved up a few feet in the line. "Sandra doesn't do anything. Ever since my nephew was born, she just stays in her room when she's not entertaining."

"That's not how I picture you at all," he grunted.

"Oh, I'm nothing like her," Anna replied. "Not that she is bad. We just like different things."

"I can understand that. Tell me more about what you do."

"Are you really interested?"

"Of course I am. Anna, I want to know all about you," he practically purred, leaning down to nuzzle her neck with his face and Anna felt the affectionate touch all the way to her toes.

Lance's eyes remained on her as they waited their turn. One large hand on her waist, the other holding their coats. She ducked her head and pressed closer to his side, liking his warmth as she told him about her job.

"Well, I do graphic design work mostly for video games. I create avatars, skins, weapons and other items like potion bottles or crowns, and I work on fantasyscapes. I did a bunch for *WolfMoon*, and *Shifter Wars*, and I did some stuff for *Secrets of the Mage*."

"Holy shit. That's awesome," he grinned. "I love those games!"

"Really? Well, I am working on a new one, *Ice Battles*. Have you heard of it?"

"No way! I have that one on preorder. I own everything Graves Enterprises puts out. In fact, I know one of their designers. He lives one town over in Barvale—Nate Cordoza."

"No way! He's a legend at GE! His avatars are so lifelike," she said, grabbing his arm in her excitement.

"Yeah, they are. He does portraits too, for friends and family. I can introduce you. Uh, maybe? Sometime, if you want, that is. He lives with his wife and kids," he added quickly. "Uh, anyway, I'd love to see some of your work."

Anna smiled and nodded. She'd never had anyone be so excited about what she did for a living. His genuine interest combined with that crazy deep voice of his was doing things to her she hardly recognized.

The sound of someone clearing their throat didn't break the look they were still sharing. The entire world seemed to fall away, and it was just the two of them.

"*Ahem.*"

But neither moved. She couldn't. It was impossible. Lance was staring into her soul. At least that was what it felt like. Casually flirtatious one moment, and serious the next. Her heart was pounding. He inched closer to her trembling form, but he wasn't alone.

Apparently, the pussy-blocking throat-clearer thought it was an invitation. But Lance did not seem the least bit disturbed. He reached out and brushed a lock of hair behind her shoulder. The touch left her shivering and oh-so-needy.

More throat clearing, followed by finger-tapping, until finally, it was accompanied by an annoyed and somewhat intrusive nasal voice.

"Excuse me."

Anna exhaled and turned her face. She felt like growling, but she held her composure. For now.

The look he'd given her was so intense. She wished she had a fan or something. A cold shower maybe? She was going to have to work to not throw herself at him. And she wasn't the only one. She noticed the woman working the coat check, eyeing him up and down like he was a snack she couldn't wait to feast on.

Hell no.

Anna frowned, then bit her lip. Truth was, it

made her nervous to think this woman, and women like her, were her competition. Tall, thin, beautiful too.

Shit.

She stole a look at Lance, but he hardly acknowledged the woman.

Relief poured through her. Lance was polite, of course. He took the ticket in his hand and stuffed it in his pants pocket with a smiled thanks. But that was it. All that crystalline blue heat flaring to life in his eyes was for Annalia alone. She smiled, calm on the outside, but firmly aware of the butterflies in her stomach. They were currently engaged in some serious mosh pit activity.

Flap, crash, flap.

Chapter Eight

Her cheeks heated and her breath caught. If she wasn't careful, she'd wind up having an asthma attack from her own nerves.

"Come on, beautiful," Lance said, taking her hand.

Anna stopped and waited for him to look at her. She needed to make things clear from the beginning, so there were no false expectations.

"You don't have to do that, you know," she said. "Call me things like baby or beautiful. I'm not expecting that—"

"Wait. Why not? Do you not like that? I would never want to offend you," he said, frowning.

"Oh, no," Anna replied. Dammit. Now she would

have to explain. "I am not offended, Lance. I just mean, I'm a realist. Men don't do that kind of thing with me. I am always the geek who gets friend-zoned by the end of the night. I just, well, before this goes any further, if that's the case, it is okay. I don't mind being your friend. I just don't want to confuse things—"

"Annalia," he said, moving closer to her, so close their fronts touched. "I don't know what kind of idiots you've dated in the past, but I am not them. I don't tell lies. I can sense them, all my people can, and I would never do that to you. It's just not in me. Hear the truth in my voice when I tell you, you take my breath away."

She was gonna melt. Right there, Anna was going to turn into a puddle of goo at his feet.

Goopy goopy goo.

Either that, or she was going to come with nothing more than a few words from this ridiculously sexy man. Her breathing grew tight. The perfume and cologne in the air made it difficult to get any air in. But that was not why her pulse was racing.

It was in the way this blue-eyed man was practically purring and running a single finger across her cheek. Like she was something precious.

"You are precious," he murmured, leaning down to brush his lips across hers in a perfectly respectable kiss. "Precious and beautiful. That's just the truth, Anna."

"Thank you," she whispered, painfully aware she'd spoken aloud again.

Sigh.

Annalia stepped back, taking a moment to collect herself. The room was gorgeous, done all in blues and silvers. The event planner had done an outstanding job with the decorations.

"It really looks like a winter wonderland in here," she mused.

"Right? I like the ice sculptures over there," Lance said, taking her cues and leading them to their designated table.

He'd nodded to the far wall where a huge forest scene was carved from ice depicting a wide array of wild animals. Impressive. Anna felt like a fairytale princess.

"They hired an orchestra too." She pointed out.

"Would you like to dance?" he asked.

Annalia did not know how much she could take of him touching her before she jumped on him, but yes, she wanted to dance. Nodding, she took a sip of the glass of water that had been waiting at her seat.

Then stood and allowed him to lead her onto the dance floor.

It was packed with beautifully dressed couples moving in time with the beat from the live band. Ladies were dressed in their finest, and men in their suits looking dashing and debonair. No one held a candle to Lance, of course, and from the look on his face, he seemed entranced by her, too.

The band began to play a beautiful arrangement of a modern dance song with their dozens of winds, string, and wood instruments, the result a spectacular rendition causing her body to vibrate.

Or was that him? Lance tugged her gently towards a dark corner of the dance floor, and she was glad. She wanted him all to herself. He sheltered her in his big embrace, heat coming off him in waves that made her shiver and quake.

Something big was happening. She couldn't put her finger on it, but it was like a magic spell, and she never wanted it to end. Anna hadn't been this turned on in forever. This kind of soul-deep craving was something she'd never experienced. It would have frightened her if she didn't see the same thing echoed in his own stare.

Concentrate on dancing, she told herself.

Easy enough with Lance leading. He moved

expertly, guiding her between the other swaying couples. Anna felt like a princess. She smiled, laughing delightfully when the crowd gasped at the sudden dimming of the lights.

"This is like magic," she said, and rested her head against his chest while he tucked her in close.

"That's just you, beautiful," his deep voice and warm breath tickled her ear.

It was all too much. She was on sensory overload. Need coursed through her veins, and Anna turned her head. But there he was. Big and handsome, and so damn close.

All she had to do was lean forward, and their lips would meet. Most of the men she'd kissed were not particularly adept at the activity. A true pity because Annalia loved to kiss.

Could be a deal breaker, she reasoned, but better to find out ahead of time.

"Won't know unless I try," she whispered.

Lance frowned but caught on as she lifted her face for him. A soft sound, like a growl, escaped his lips before he brushed her mouth with his once, then twice.

The light, teasing touches were driving her mad. She licked her lips. Not because she was trying to be seductive, but because she wanted, needed more pressure.

Lance was a fast learner. His lips pressed against hers in a hot and hard crush. He held her closer still, flooding her with his heat. One hand on her waist, the other on her cheek, Lance slid his tongue inside her mouth, dominating her with his seductive skill.

Sirens were going off like mad inside of her. If Anna wasn't careful, she would be confessing her undying love for the man after one single kiss.

Why not? It had happened for her parents that way. Love at first sight. But things like that didn't happen anymore, the reasonable side of her brain said blandly.

They do now, she thought and threw herself into the moment. She'd never been kissed like that. Never had the world stand still and tremble at the same time while fireworks went off in the sky.

He was branding her with his lips, ruining her for anyone else, marking her with his tongue. Lance's kiss was changing the way she would think about kisses forevermore. She was gasping for air by the time he lifted his head. And Anna was gratified to see. So was he.

"Anna," he whispered her name.

"Hello Lance, Annalia, I see you arrived safe and sound," a familiar voice interrupted them.

Anna raised her shocked face to see Uncle Uzzi dancing alongside them with a beautiful, silver-haired woman. The older man was resplendent in a white tuxedo, blue eyes sparkling with glee.

"Uncle Uzzi!" Annalia couldn't stop herself from smiling widely. "Are you having an enjoyable time?"

"Yes, of course. You look beautiful, dear. And, Lance, how are you doing?"

"Good evening, Uncle Uzzi," Lance said, and his eyes flashed gold for a second when he looked at Anna.

"I see. Well, Lance, Annalia, I hope you have a good night."

Uncle Uzzi's eyes seemed vacant for a moment as he answered. A moment later, he nodded, and spun his dance partner away. Lance was still grinning when he turned to Anna.

"Can I ask you a question, Lance?"

"Of course," he said. "You can ask me anything."

"Let's stop dancing a moment."

"Sure. Come on."

Lance led her off the floor. White flower arrangements with pale blue ribbons adorning them sat on several of the tall tables surrounding the dance floor. There had to be four hundred people in the large space, and suddenly Annalia's chest squeezed tight.

She hated crowds. The flowers, the perfume, her nerves, everything was adding up and breathing was growing difficult. Of course, her pump was in her clutch. The very one she'd checked with her coat at the entrance. She would be okay, Anna just had to take it easy.

Slow it down, she scolded herself. Last thing she wanted was to cause a scene.

"Can I get you something, Annalia? A drink?"

"Please," Anna responded, and placed her palms flat on the table.

Lance looked worried. She wanted to tell him not to be, but right then, she had other things to do.

Like breathe.

He hailed a passing server. Snagging a glass of champagne from the tray, he handed it to her. Anna nodded her thanks, sipping the chilled wine to soothe her frayed nerves.

"Anna, do you want to go?"

"No. I apologize, I just got winded."

"You never have to apologize to me. You said you wanted to ask me something?"

"Yeah, *uh*, why did you hire Uncle Uzzi to find you a date?"

"What?"

"Well, look at you. I mean, you're completely hot, and from the moment we walked into this place, dozens of women have been giving you come hither looks. So, obviously you aren't struggling for female attention," she said and noticed a striking blonde headed their way. Anna rolled her eyes.

"For example," Annalia sighed and pointed.

"Excuse me," the blonde said smiling at Lance, she looked at Anna like she was a bug under her shoe and practically pushed her out of her way.

"Lance, my love," the stranger stage whispered.

Her slim figure was decked out in a skintight dress that showed off not an ounce of fat. Red fingernails reached out and grabbed his lapels as the woman pressed her body against his.

Anna's whole being tensed. She couldn't help but stare at the scene as it played out. So, this was his usual date. Made perfect sense. She hardly knew him, had no reason to be hurt, and yet Anna felt like her heart was being torn in two.

Maybe he would push her away? Maybe he would explain the blonde bombshell mistook him for someone else? But no. Anna watched Lance's expression. Red-faced, like he'd been caught double-dipping. Yes, he was more than uncomfortable. He looked guilty.

Oh no.

She wanted to yell, to scream. What an idiot she'd been, building castles out of a dance. This was a mistake. Talking to Uncle Uzzi, agreeing to the makeover, coming here had all been a terrible mistake. Anna didn't even have to listen to the simpering female to know she was right.

"Brenda, not now," he growled.

"I know what this is, Lance. We've been through this before," the woman said with a scathing look at Annalia. "I know you want to make me jealous by dancing with another woman, and you win, I am jealous. Now come on, let's makeup," she said, dropping her voice to a sultry whisper that made Anna want to puke.

"Move," he growled at the woman, but Anna wasn't buying it.

If he'd wanted to move, he would have stepped away from her grasping hands, but he didn't. Anna's dreams came crashing down fast as Lance remained right where he was with that woman's hands all over him.

Jerk.

"Don't play hard to get, Lance-a-lot. I said, I was sorry about leaving the other morning when I texted you. Didn't you see it? Let's get out of here. I'll make you forget all about that silly little fight. You know I can. I got what you need, Lance."

The woman's voice was loud now, and Anna was desperate to get away, but the couple had her exit blocked off. She was trapped, watching her so-called date and his real girlfriend have their little romantic makeup scene.

Shit.

Humiliation was not a good look on Anna, and she was already cursing herself ten times a fool for falling for his lines. Thank goodness she hadn't gone home with him. She always fell too hard too fast.

Shifters, magic, whatever.

There was nothing special for her here. Her breathing became strained as her emotions grew even more volatile. This was stupid. She was stupid.

"Excuse me," Anna said, and tried to get around them, but neither moved.

"Is this why you wouldn't text me back all day, Lance? For this chubby little nobody?" The bitch laughed.

"Don't talk to her, Brenda," Lance growled, and

there was no trace of blue left in his eyes as they flashed to Anna. Only the gold of his Tiger.

"Really? She's human, Lance, what can she do for you?" Brenda the bitch hissed. "Look, I don't know who you are, but me and Lance have a relationship that spans years—"

"All in the past," he growled, but Anna did not want to hear it.

Thunder roared in her ears as embarrassment washed over her. Sandra was right all along. It didn't matter what she wore, she had nothing to offer a man. Especially one who looked like that. She should have known better.

But so should he. What the hell was he thinking? Kissing her and dancing with her like she was the only person who existed. How was she supposed to know he'd been playing some revenge game?

"I just want to leave," she murmured.

"No, Anna—"

"Let her leave, Lance."

His inhuman growl was too loud for the humans near them, and Brenda looked around nervously. Anna wanted to help, but she couldn't/ Brenda was right. She was just a human.

"Anna," he pleaded.

But she shook her head, she could not speak to

him. Yes, she wanted to believe it was all a mistake, but the woman obviously knew him. Lance wasn't even trying to deny her claim. He was looking from Anna to the stranger, but he was silent. Tongue-tied and red-faced as fuck.

That could only mean one thing. He'd spent the night with this Brenda and recently too. This whole date was probably some kind of pity revenge thing. A favor he owed Uncle Uzzi, maybe?

Anna was fuming. She did not need or want anyone's pity. She deserved better. Screw Sandra, and Glenn. And screw Lance too.

He might be handsome, but he was just another liar, and Anna had no time for that in her life. Humiliation rolled off her in waves. It might sting for a while, but she would do better next time. She just needed to find a ride back to the cabin.

No way was she standing around, waiting for Lance to finish his little reunion.

Fuck that.

"I'm getting out of here," she said firmly, and pushed past the couple.

Chapter Nine

"Brenda, get the fuck off me," Lance growled.

Finally, he found his fucking voice. Anna had just stormed off, and he could not blame her one bit. She deserved an explanation, and she was going to get one. As soon as he rid himself of this vengeful, she-Cat.

"Don't call me. Don't contact me. And do not ever touch me again. I found my mate, and it is not you," he growled with his Tiger barely contained.

Fucking fuck.

He didn't even know the female would be there tonight. The woman was a troublemaker and probably finagled a ticket from some unknowing schmuck. But why she thought he'd be interested was beyond him.

His Tiger snarled, scratching against his skin. He didn't want her anywhere near him. When she'd pushed his sweet Anna aside, he almost went nuts. The female had her claws on his chest before he could get his Tiger under control.

It was touch and go, but finally, he'd managed to rein in the beast. Only it was too late. Anna had walked away. The stiff set of her shoulders told him he'd fucked up. He had no wish to harm Brenda, but she needed to get the fuck off him now.

"What the heck, Lance?" Brenda pouted.

"Move," he growled. "Annalia!"

Lance called after her, moving around Brenda. He dismissed the she-Tiger without a backwards glance. Where did Anna go?

His beast roared angrily. Pissed that he'd allowed Brenda to put her hands on him. Even more pissed that Anna had stormed away. The scent of her hurt and anger clawed at him. Fuck, he had to make this right.

"Lance, what happened?" Uncle Uzzi came growling his way, and it was all he could do not to bowl the Witch over. "Where is Anna?"

"Uncle Uzzi, I fucked up. She walked away. Fuck!"

He pulled on his hair, and turned his head,

sucking in air to try and catch her scent. There were too many smells, though. Too much perfume and shit.

"Dammit! She's my mate. She doesn't understand. Brenda touched me, Uncle Uzzi. My Tiger was so enraged, I couldn't move," he growled, and tried to move around him, but the stubborn man wouldn't budge.

"I see, and do you think you are in any shape now to go after her? You look like you're hunting a gazelle. Get a hold of yourself," Uncle Uzzi snapped his fingers, and blue sparks zapped him.

Ouch.

"Need my mate," he rumbled, fangs protruding from his mouth.

"For fuck's sake, control your beast. Come now, move, Lance" He said and grabbed him by the arm.

Uzzi pulled him towards the back of the gala. Luckily, almost ninety percent of those in attendance were Shifters or their mates. If he went furry, there wouldn't be a huge scandal.

Just a teeny weeny one. Pussy.

Lance growled. His Tiger was a fucking jerk sometimes.

Fuck you, dick. If there was a scandal, it would be fucking HUGE.

Grrr.

Lance was losing his grip on his Tiger. He'd upset his sweet Annalia. That damned she-Cat had touched him and he froze. It was all he could do to stop his beast from reacting with claws and fangs.

A roaring snarl went through him and he felt fur peppering his cheeks, his animal this close to ripping out of him Then it hit him. The scent of chocolate and spiced cherries had him stopping in his tracks.

Annalia.

Mine.

The sound of her familiar voice both soothed and agitated him further. She sounded different, both breathless and annoyed. The combination confused him as he stalked towards the direction her voice was coming from.

"Where are you running off to, little one?"

"Yeah, a sweet little piece like you should be on the dance floor with someone like me. What do ya say?"

It was two men from a local Hyena Pack. Those bottom-dwelling pieces of shit did not belong here. And they certainly did not belong touching his mate.

"Ex-excuse me, I-I am t-trying t-to leave," she was gasping her words.

He frowned. It was like she couldn't get enough air. Lance stalked towards them, her gaze darting from the two soon to be dead assholes and back to him like she didn't know which option was worse. That hurt, but he supposed he deserved it.

Her sudden pallor worried him. Had he done this to her? Fear and anger raged through him. Mostly at himself. But some of it was aimed at the two fuckers who were standing way too close to her.

The larger of the pair of Hyena Shifters lifted a lock of her hair and bent down to sniff. That was all it took. Lance saw red.

"Lance," Uncle Uzzi cautioned, but he was too far gone.

"Mine," he leapt across the hall, and had both men by their throats.

The Hyenas were strong, but no match for his enormous beast. Especially when his animal was so enraged. He shook the men, snarling ferociously.

"Annalia! Your pump?" Uncle Uzzi asked his mate, snaring his attention.

The old Witch raced towards the coat check when his mate pointed in that direction.

Pump? Oh shit.

Now it made sense. He turned back to the two struggling assholes and banged them together once to get their attention.

"Get gone," Lance snarled, pushing the men back.

He ran to where Anna had pressed herself against the wall, crouching in front of her, hands raised.

Fuck, she was scared. Her face was ashen. Tears streamed down her face. Lance had never felt so helpless and frightened in his life. Her scent was sharp.

Hurt, discomfort, fear.

Her emotions batted against him, a thousand blows he more than deserved. And he took them all one by one.

Fuck.

He was a total piece of shit.

"I'm sorry, so sorry. Please baby, I won't hurt you. Never hurt you," he murmured. "Just gonna get you help. You can tell me to fuck off afterwards, but I need you to be okay, first."

Lance lifted her off the floor. He rushed to where Uncle Uzzi was currently rummaging through the closet to find her coat.

"It's the black one," Lance told the Witch, cradling his precious cargo close as he sat down on the bench rubbing her back in large circles with his left hand.

"Look at me, love, it's okay. You're okay. Slowly, now, you can do this." Lance breathed in and out, setting a pace for her to follow, and whispering words of praise when she echoed the motion.

She had some color back, but she was still wheezing. He felt helpless. Stupid. A total asshole. And he was all those things, in that order, too.

"Here." Uncle Uzzi tossed her medicine to him, and Lance plucked it out of the air with his right hand.

"Here, love," he held the pump up, shook it once, and she leaned forward to suck in as he pressed on it.

Annalia inhaled the medicine greedily, trembling slightly in his arms like a flower petal at the mercy of a winter storm.

Just as beautiful and delicate, too. She nodded and he held up the pump.

"Again?"

Another nod.

He understood. Lance shook the pump one more time and pressed the medicine into her mouth. Finally, after some minutes, she was breathing calmly.

"Thank you," her raspy voice met his ears, and he closed his eyes.

She was okay. No thanks to him.

"Annalia, I—"

He wanted to explain, but she shook her head and turned to Uncle Uzzi. He felt her tremble, knew she was weak and hurting. All because of him.

Fuck. Fuck. Fuck.

"Uncle Uzzi," her voice sounded rough as she spoke to the other male, ignoring Lance. "Can you take me back?"

"Of course," Uncle Uzzi told her, sparing one sharp glare at Lance. He took Annalia's hand, and helped her stand. Then the male led his mate away.

It was too much, too soon. He'd met and lost his mate in the span of a few hours. Lance's Tiger clawed furiously against his skin. The beast wanted out.

Fuck.

Lance took off outside, allowing his Tiger to surge forward. He raced towards the woods that lined the parking lot, shredding his suit to pieces as his Shift took hold.

The nine-hundred-pound beast that lived inside of him was completely enraged. He'd lost his mate tonight and the knowledge might drive him mad.

He felt her though. She was close, but too far to see. Too far to smell. Uncle Uzzi had her in his car and that was good. He would protect her.

Lance should've killed those Hyena fucks for

touching her, but she was safe from them now. He wished he could blame the asthma attack on them, but he knew better.

Lance was responsible. Brenda had caught him off guard and he was not in control enough to react. Anna was human. She wouldn't have understood his struggle to control his Tiger. Worthy males did not strike out against females, and repulsive as he found Brenda's behavior, she had *once upon a time* been a friend.

She was nothing to him now. Her behavior was completely unforgiveable. Lance's Tiger snarled at the thought of the haughty she-Cat.

Uncle Uzzi had her in the metal and glass machine. Anna was in there, and at that very moment, she was moving away from him faster than his Tiger could calculate. Still, the beast gave chase.

Snarling loudly, Lance pushed his long, muscular, feline body hard through the forest that lined the highway. He needed to know she was safe, to see it with his own eyes.

She'd been struggling to breathe, and he hadn't known why.

Asthma.

His sweet mate had asthma, a very dangerous condition if not addressed. Clearly, she had meds, but if he'd known about it, he would've turned down the tickets Uzzi had offered. He would have taken her somewhere with less people, less perfume, less flowers. Less chance of running into Brenda.

Fuck.

He'd fucked this all up. He roared into the night, landing on the snow-covered ground for split seconds before taking off once more. Pushing himself, he followed the sedan from his path among the trees. Until finally, it turned off the highway, into a hidden driveway. Then it stopped.

Good. Home.

Lance waited as his mate exited the vehicle. The driver did not touch her, good thing too. Before he could stop himself, his beast pushed, and he leapt onto the porch as she'd finished waving goodbye to Uncle Uzzi. The car was already driving away, by the time she turned and saw him.

Fuck. She was beautiful as she mounted the stairs. He kept getting little teasing peeks of her legs through the slit of her gown. The red dress had looked amazing on her, and he could only imagine how much better it would look on the floor while he had her splayed and nude atop of the king sized mattress inside his cabin. The fact she was staying there soothed his beast, and he chuffed as she approached him warily.

Mine. My mate.

"Lance?" she questioned, and silly beast that he was, he closed his eyes, savoring the sound of his name on her lips.

Contrary to his nature, his animal—*completely at ease in her presence*—let his guard down and inhaled the sultry sweet spice that was her delicious scent. Of course, the Tiger hadn't expected the sweet female to brain him with one of the large metal pokers he had hanging over the outdoor chiminea.

Yowl.

"Go back home to your girlfriend and stop stalking me, you two-timing jerk!"

Annalia turned around and Lance sat there and shook his head. Fuck, that hurt. Okay, so he had followed her home, but he wasn't a stalker. Maybe. Not yet anyway. Fuck.

He had just wanted her to be safe. Lance stood up on four legs, albeit a little shakily, and chuffed at his mate while she struggled with the keycode. Her breath hitched in her throat, and he growled worriedly.

Surely, she could tell he was there for her. Of course, his beast's understanding of women was a little more one-dimensional than his human side. Meaning, the Cat expected her to know she belonged to him and act accordingly. He pressed his head against her rear, wanting her attention on him.

Fuck. She was crying. His Tiger growled softly, wanting to ease her pain, but the woman was not having any of that. She spun around, poker still in hand, and smashed it over his skull for the second time in as many minutes.

Pain exploded in his head and for one single moment, Lance's beast saw two women who looked very much like his Anna, standing before him, looking furious and beautiful. Her lip trembled, and he knew he deserved both blows, but all he wanted to do was comfort her. He felt his change wash over him and in the blink of an eye, he stood before her in his skin, raising his arm when she would have hit him a third time.

"Anna, please, you have to listen—"

"I don't have to do anything. Now, back off you two-timing pussy!"

Chapter Ten

L ance shook his entire body against the cold as he swapped fur for skin.

"Fuck! That hurt."

He raised his free hand in surrender still gripping the poker she was holding onto after her third attempt to smash his skull in. the woman was strong, and spunky too. Good for her.

She should be pissed, and he knew she was even without the way she was squinting her eyes angrily. It was the tear tracks on her face that broke his heart. Nothing he said was going to be good enough.

"Please don't cry," he murmured. "I know I do not deserve another chance, Anna. But I am asking for one. Please, Annalia. But I won't be able to explain if I am passed out with a concussion," he began, and she had to hide the twitch of her lips. "First, I'm so sorry. I swear, I never want to hurt you. Not ever."

"Okay, but maybe we should talk later," she mumbled. Her face was turning the same shade as her dress, and he cocked his head to the side. Then, she squeaked and looked down.

"Dude, you're naked. Your jingle berries are just flapping in the breeze here, and well, I can't take you seriously—"

Fuck, she was cute. Lance felt his dick grow hard under her perusal and Anna gasped and her eyes went wide with shock and something else. Maybe interest?

Please let it be interest.

"OMG. You have a boner!" she squeaked and covered her eyes with her hands.

Lance stood taller, unashamed of his nudity. Shifters were used to it, but what sweetened the deal was the heady scent of her arousal floating on the breeze. The winter night was cold, and she was starting to shiver.

"Hear me out, Anna. Let's go inside so you're not cold. I promise I won't do anything unless you tell me to. You have my word."

"Your word?"

"You might not think much of it right now, but

it's the best thing I can give you. I swear it. Look, leave the door open if you want, but you're shivering, and my Tiger is going crazy inside of me wanting to get you inside. Safe. Warm," he growled, and she stood there a moment before nodding.

"Alright," she said, trusting him enough to turn her back on him as she entered the code correctly.

"You can shut the door," she said, walking to the other side of the room, poker in hand.

Fine. She could have that. She could have anything she wanted far as he was concerned.

Anna's gaze flicked to his cock for a moment, and the damn thing stirred again. She whimpered, eyes wide, and flashing back to his. He shrugged.

"I can't help that, Anna. You keep looking at me, I'm gonna get hard."

"Cause Shifters are horn balls with no control?" she asked.

He shook his head. Silly woman. Didn't she know it had nothing to do with sex and everything to do with her?

"Not at all, Anna. It's cause you're the one doing the looking."

hat the what now?

Anger and lust warred with each other, the latter winning out by a smidge. The tall, gorgeous, and naked—*did she mention naked*—man had followed her home in his Tiger form, and now, the giant was standing in her rented living room.

Did she say giant?

Cause dayum. When she said that, Anna meant GIANT.

Had to be at least eleven semi-hard inches so far, and it was still growing every time her gaze brushed along his impressive and girthy length. She rolled her eyes to the ceiling and huffed out a breath.

She could do this. Have a conversation with a gorgeous naked ass man that she felt completely possessive over after less than two hours of his company for no rational reason at all, right? Sure she could. Anna was an adult.

"First, I'm naked because we can't shift with clothes on," he explained.

"Alright but does that always happen when you Shift?" wide-eyed she pointed at his now loud and proud full on erection.

Not that he had no reason to be proud, she reasoned.

One more time with feeling—the man had earned it.

Dayum, she thought.

Wait, that wasn't enough. Okay. DAYUM!

That was more like it.

"No," he growled, gripping his enormous dick with one hand. "Like I said, this," he grumbled and stroked himself from root to tip, "is all because of you."

"Things like that don't happen cause of me," she confessed.

"They sure as fuck do, Anna."

She shook her head, mesmerized by the way he was touching himself, groaning when he stopped. When her gaze met his, she found his sexy grin had faded. Lance stalked forward, backing her into the wall. He reached up removing her jacket, letting it drop to the floor. His blue eyes on hers the entire time as he grazed his fingertips across her shoulders, waiting for her reaction before pressing his body close.

She hardly noticed she'd been shivering with cold, and maybe something else, but the second he touched her she felt it. His warmth. Despite his nakedness, Lance was a raging inferno.

"You're hot," she murmured against his chest.

"So are you," he returned.

"No, I mean like literally," she said with an unladylike snort and rolled her eyes. "Your skin is hot."

"Oh, that's just a Shifter thing."

"We should be talking, Lance. Not doing this," she murmured as he ran his lips along her neck and jawline.

"You're right. Of course," he growled, and when he looked at her his eyes were the gold of his beast. "If it makes you more comfortable, I can put something on while we talk, Anna."

She sighed, knowing she was going to listen to what he had to say. She needed to. Maybe she was being a fool or easy, but something inside her told her she would regret it for the rest of her life if she pushed him away now.

"Okay," she said and stepped away from his warmth. "But I don't think I have anything that fits you."

"No worries, I keep spare clothes in the back hall closet."

"Wait. What? You keep clothes *here*?"

He was bending down and lifting her coat off the floor, sidestepping the question as he hung it on the rack by the door. Lance, bent down again, lifting her feet and removing her heels almost immediately.

Fuck, that felt good. How did he know she needed them off? Dressing up like Cinderella for the night, didn't mean she'd changed. Anna was a creature of habit, and that meant comfort was king.

"This is my cabin," Lance explained after guiding her to the sofa.

"Your cabin?"

"Yeah, I own it. Actually, I built it. I only stay here half the time though. My beast has been anxious lately. Anyway, Uncle Uzzi asked to use it," he explained and walked to the hall closet where he expertly removed a pair of gray sweatpants from the bottom drawer and shrugged them on.

Chest still bare, the ripple of muscles playing across his body was hypnotic. Anna had to bite back her groan, and she did, literally taking her lower lip between her teeth. Lance seemed to follow the movement, eyes narrowing as he walked back over to her.

"If you want to be bitten, love, you just have to ask," Lance growled and bent down, placing himself between her legs, then proceeded to kiss the hell out of her.

Annalia whimpered at the first thrust of his

tongue. Had she made jokes about him not being a good kisser, because the man was a damn expert. Fuck how he got that way. She didn't want to know about the years of practice he'd had, only cared about the way he was handling her right then.

So good.

She really shouldn't be doing this, but his big warm body was pressed up against hers, his cock pulsing against the apex of her thighs.

"What are you doing? We're supposed to be talking."

But she didn't push him away. She couldn't. Fuck. He felt so good. His big body pushing against hers, and it had been so long since anyone had made her feel that way—*if ever.*

"Can't help it. You smell so fucking good. Like sex and sweet spice. Want you," growled and sniffed the crook of her neck.

Moisture pooled between her legs. Anna whimpered. The snow in his hair had melted, and it his chestnut locks were damp and curling against his forehead and neck. She couldn't help herself. Annalia reached up, pushing them back, pulling his face closer to her skin. He growled as he kissed her neck, then moved back to her lips, and down the other side of her neck.

He was driving her crazy with those small nuzzles. Each tentative touch made her shiver with need and want. His entire chest vibrated against her with the sound. Lance's warm, minty breath mingled with hers. Anticipation—*not asthma*—had her breath catching in her throat.

She wanted his lips, wanted his tongue. Panting with the strength of her need, she nuzzled his cheek. Lance turned, stroking his nose against hers, teasing her mouth with his lips.

Hardly touching, and yet she moaned anyway. Those tiny whispers of kisses made her want to weep in frustration.

"Lance," she moaned.

"What do you want, Anna? Tell me."

"Kiss me," she demanded.

"I am," he grinned.

The bastard.

"No," she growled, biting his lip, hard. "Stop fucking around and kiss me."

The deep, throaty growl that rumbled through his chest until it escaped his lips shouldn't have made her panties wet—*okay, soaked*—but it did. Anna's muscles seemed to lock in place. She was a deer caught in the path of a dangerous predator.

Lance was that and more, a true Tiger inside and

out. She didn't know if this was smart, risking her heart with a man like him, all for the sake of a night's pleasure.

Suddenly, Lance reached up with both hands cupping her face. He angled her head exactly where he wanted. Then he kissed her.

For real, this time. Lance thrust his tongue inside her mouth, and Anna forgot why she'd been worried to begin with.

OMG...yes, yes, YASSSSS!

This was what she'd been missing in her life. A man who knew exactly what to do with a woman like her. She moaned into his mouth, but he didn't let up. Thank fuck.

Anna might kick herself tomorrow, but right then she was going to take everything he offered. And nothing mattered in that moment except his mouth on hers. He spent countless time, licking and nibbling at her lips, exploring her entire mouth, teeth, tongue, all of it.

He kissed, teased, licked, and breathed her in. As if he could swallow her very essence down with a single, though incredible, kiss. Meanwhile, his hands held her face in the gentlest of caresses. She clutched his shoulders, using his hard body for support. God knew she had no strength in her legs.

The man gave the phrase 'weak in the knees' new meaning.

"Too many clothes," she ground out against his insistent mouth.

"You sure?" he panted the question and bent to kiss her again.

Anna moaned, lips still locked with his. Something primal inside her was gratified he seemed as out of breath as she was.

"Yes, I'm sure."

Anna grinned and pushed him back with two hands on his chest. She knew he was the stronger of the two, but he allowed her to move him.

That alone was hot as fuck, far as she was concerned. The man was sex on legs, but she was in charge.

Watching her like a true predator, he followed every move she made as if mesmerized. The knowledge gave her a little power trip, and she shook her head when he made to move.

"Not till I say," Anna whispered, moving away from the sofa.

Lance growled but remained where she left him. Somehow, they'd made out across the sofa till they were both on the floor. Anna stood up, eyeing his thick erection beneath the gray sweats he'd pulled on. His cock seemed to beg for attention. But not yet, she told herself.

Anna continued to walk backwards, tugging the zipper under her left arm that held the strapless dress up.

"Want me to take this off?"

"Fuck yeah," he nodded.

"You can start walking," she told him, gasping at how quickly he stood and stalked her. "Stop," she said when he almost reached her. "No touching. Not until I say so."

"Anything you want, love," he growled, eyes focused like laser beams.

The feline grace with which he moved was not lost on her. She marveled at how such a big man held so much elegance in his every move. He was big, muscular, sexy, and beautiful. The issues she had, they could work out later. Right then, she was on fire for him.

Anna's eyes never left his, but she didn't need to see where she was going. The beauty of the cabin was in its open design. Entryway, hall, kitchen to the left, living room, then a single door that led to the master bedroom and bath. There was a soft rug beneath her feet as she passed the fireplace and the sofa. Mindful of where she stepped, Anna held the now unzipped dress high.

Lance's growl grew in volume when she paused just in front of the bedroom door. One hand on the doorknob, still facing him, Anna dropped the dress. His breath whooshed out on a loud exhale, and she was so fucking glad she went with the black lace lingerie.

The demi-cup bustier lifted her large breasts while the see-through fabric hid nothing from the eye. The matching panties made her feel sexy, naughty, and the way his eyes ate her bolstered her confidence a little more. His gaze turned gold, zeroing in on her already slick sex.

"See anything you like?" she teased.

"Mine."

The word was barely recognizable, but so fucking hot coming from his mouth. Lance's body was tensed, his muscles gleaming in the dimmed lighting of the bedroom.

Annalia turned around, not missing the way he sucked in another breath. She walked over to the king-sized bed and stood in front of it.

"You coming?"

"You first," he grunted the words.

<h1 style="text-align:center">Chapter Eleven</h1>

"If we do this, we are starting something you may not want, Annalia," Lance said, voice thick with his Tiger.

The beast wanted to shred him for even giving her an out but fuck his animal. Annalia had a right to know exactly what she was getting into. His beast was possessive, ornery, and he wanted her more with each passing minute.

Annalia smiled then. Her grin so real and wide, honest, and open, he felt his heart *thump, thump, thump* inside his chest.

Lance pounced. There was no other word for it, really. He wrapped her in his arms, spinning her around and crushing his mouth over hers.

Shivers of arousal zoomed up and down his spine

at the slightest touch. But this, this was so much more than that. Lance was hot and hard, and so fucking ready for her, he fucking ached. His body trembled like a green cub as she pushed his sexy gray sweats out of the way. Her small hand closed around his hardened shaft, and he went cross-eyed at how good she felt around him.

"Need to be in you," he grunted the words.

Then he had her pressed so tightly to his body he could barely breathe. Who needed air, anyway? Lance started kissing her again, and it was amazing. Anna moaned, but the sound was lost in his mouth. He swallowed it down, devouring her. With claw-tipped fingers he cut the bustier from her body.

"I am sorry," he apologized.

Why was he apologizing?

Like seriously, he just wanted to get the fucking thing off already. Lingerie was sexy, but nothing compared to Anna. Her body was a wonderland he could not way to discover for himself. Cupping her sex, he growled and nibbled her neck, loving the feel of her nails as she clung to his shoulders.

"I'll buy you another set. I'll buy you a hundred. Just need to touch you."

For a moment, Annalia thought Lance was going to stop his sensual assault and apologize for what had transpired earlier that night.

Talk about a mood killer, and Anna really didn't want to talk about that now. She did not want to think of Lance with other women, especially not that female who had her paws all over him.

All Anna wanted was for him to keep doing that thing he was doing with his mouth. Oh wow. Yes.

"Yeah, that. Keep doing that. THAT RIGHT THERE!"

"Anything you want," he told her, and she was flying so high, Anna did not even care she'd spoken aloud again.

"Oh god," she tossed her head back as his lips found her chest.

Capturing her nipple in his hot mouth, he tugged on the tiny bud, scraping it with his fang. Anna held on to his arms, trying desperately to bring his mouth back to her other breast. As if he could read her mind, he was there a moment later, and her pussy dripped cream down her thighs.

"I can scent your need. Like chocolate cherries

and spice. So fucking good. So mine," he pressed her down into the bed, and she went willingly.

Nodding her head jerkily, Anna moved back onto the plush comforter, feet down, and knees high. Lance's eyes glowed with his Tiger as they raked over her naked body.

Modesty had no place here. Not between them. Lance placed his gigantic hands on the insides of her knees, then he pressed them apart. Cool air danced along her overheated flesh.

"Look at you, so pretty and pink," he growled and licked his lips. "So perfect."

Holy shit.

He was looking at her down there, staring at her sex like it held the answers to the universe, and fuck, if that didn't move her another step closer to coming. Bending forward, eyes locked on hers, Lance dropped an open-mouthed kiss right on her pussy. Growling with hunger, he lapped at her sex until Anna saw stars.

"Want you to come on my tongue, Anna," he growled and ran his fingers along the seam of her sex.

Fuck, yes, She wanted that too. Anna couldn't talk. She only nodded. Lucky for her, Lance was not finished talking.

Thank god.

He spread her cream around, using his thumbs to massage her sensitive lips before spearing her on his middle and index finger.

"So wet for me, baby. Good girl. Taste like heaven," he growled and licked her from her forbidden hole to her clit, sucking the bundle of nerves into his mouth while he stretched her with his digits.

"Oh god, yes," she moaned.

"Want you to be mine, Anna. Want that?"

"Yes," she nodded.

"Mine," he growled, licking, and sucking harder.

Her heavy breathing filled the air, but again, this was not because of Anna's asthma. She didn't need her inhaler. No, what she needed was to come.

Fuck, she pushed against his mouth.

The stinging invasion of yet another finger filling her gave her just the edge she needed. He sucked her clit, hard, harder, all the while fucking her with his fingers. She was going to come any second now.

Please, please, please come, she begged herself.

Her body worked in tandem with his. Striving, pursuing, chasing down her release.

"Gonna fill you with my cock, baby. Gonna fuck you so good, you just have to come first," he growled.

Anna lifted herself up on her elbows. She

watched him eating her pussy. Met his gaze as he lifted his face, mouth coated with her juices.

Lance held her stare, lapping at her clit in long, broad strokes. Faster and faster.

So fucking hot, she thought and pressed her pussy against his tongue, rocking her hips in time with his thrusts.

Yes, more, yes, harder.

"Oh fuck," she moaned, and her mind went numb.

All she could see, breathe, hear was him as he sucked and licked her clit. His thick fingers pushed in and out of her sheath, bringing her orgasm to fruition.

"Now, now," she ground herself against him. A deep, throaty moan was ripped from her lips.

Anna's entire body was on fire with pleasure. Then he was sliding up her legs, pressing them wide, crawling up the bed. His big cock in his hand, he placed the tip between her legs, kissing her soaked entrance with his mushroomed head.

"Watch me push inside you," he growled, "Look at us, Annalia."

Fuck, she loved that he called her by name.

She reared up on her elbows, watching as he

pushed his thick cock into her slick heat. He felt so good.

Her body was stretched like a rubber band, so tense, so tight. Any second now she was going to snap apart.

"I'll hold you together," he growled against her neck, "Never let you go."

"Lance!" she yelled as sensations she'd never felt before spiraled down her body. "Please."

She begged for things she didn't even understand. Her body was trying to tell her something, and she wanted to give it to herself. To have him all for herself. Yes, that's what it was.

The steel length of him stroked her inside, so much thicker, longer than his hand. He slid even deeper, coaxing reactions from her she'd never felt. Anna thought she'd reached heaven before, but she was wrong.

How could she have when his cock was only now sliding along her g-spot? That incredible appendage rubbed her so good, filled her exactly right, drove her into another wave of rapturous bliss.

Her small nails cut into his shoulders as she lifted herself up, encouraging him to move faster. With her legs tight around his waist, she forced him to go deeper.

"Fuck," he growled, "don't wanna hurt you."

"You won't hurt me. I want more, Lance, I want it all," she demanded.

And he gave it. Fuck, did he give. Lance roared, his Tiger glowing from his eyes as he pounded into her. The stretching of her walls as she tried to encompass his thick length burned so damn good.

The feelings spiraling through her were too delicious for words. His body was a finely tuned machine. When his lips were within reach, she caught them with her own, reveling in the meeting of lips, tongues, and even teeth on sensitive skin.

Sweat coated their bodies, and the sounds of skin slapping against skin echoed in the cabin. This was not the sweet and tender lovemaking she'd envisioned when she'd first seen him. This was rough and raw, and she loved every fucking second of it.

"Now," he growled, closing his jaws over her skin.

Sharp pain shattered her bliss, but was soon replaced by an orgasm so explosive, she actually saw stars. Whole universes, in fact. All of them dying and being born in the space of an instant. A scream tore from her throat, echoed by his resounding roar as Lance arched his back.

Hot jets of cum filled her pussy until it was dripping down her thighs, but still he rocked his hips, and her orgasm went on and on. Aftershocks rippled through the two of them for several minutes. Anna was speechless, breathless. Hell, all she could do was hold him in place.

Soul-deep pleasure was not something she was used to. Fucking hell, she was surprised she even recognized it.

But this was it, Anna thought with an exhausted grin.

Chapter Twelve

Lance was still catching his breath, and he glanced down at Annalia to check she was okay, heart squeezing tight when he found her with the most endearing smile on her face.

She looked so beautiful like that. All pink with exertion, and breathless, but not dangerously so. She looked happy, sated, and well-loved. Lance could not help but continue to kiss her, touch her, everywhere he could. He refused to slide out of her, not yet. He wanted to prolong their connection for as many minutes as she allowed.

Lucky him, his Anna did not seem inclined to release him either. Her hands traced his back, arms, and chest, and around again to his ass. He dipped his head to her lips, kissing her softly, gently, drinking her in and memorizing every nuance of her sweet and spicy flavor.

Tomorrow they would finish their talk and Lance would explain everything that had happened with Brenda. He would tell her all of it. But mostly, he would confess his feelings for her, because fast or not, Lance Jacosa was in love for the first time in his life.

Annalia was the most important thing in the world to him and starting tomorrow he was going to show her.

"Where is she?"

"Excuse me?" Uncle Uzzi practically barked over the phone.

Hell, the Witch would probably chew him out over his insolence, but Lance was beside himself. After the best, most poignant night of his life, Lance dozed off with dreams of the future dancing in his brain, to wake up completely alone.

He'd claimed Annalia as his mate, then she'd walked out on him, leaving the cabin with all her belongings. No note. No text. Nothing. She was gone without a trace.

Fucking hell.

He'd been in some post-claiming coma, and she'd up and headed out of Dodge. His Tiger yowled and roared unhappily. The beast enraged he'd done something to make her leave.

"Lance, what is going on? Are you with Anna?" Uzzi asked.

"I was. I mean, I followed you both back to the cabin last night, and we, uh, that is—"

"Oh Lance! You claimed that human girl without explaining what it means! Do any of you pussies listen to a word I say? I swear, Hunter and I need to call a Pride meeting if I am going to continue to work with you boneheaded Tiger Shifters!"

"I apologize. Sincerely, I do, but Uncle Uzzi, I need my mate. Do you know where she is?" Lance asked, his voice hoarse.

"Of course, I know where she is. But I am not telling you," the old Witch scoffed. "Not until you calm down and think this through like you should have from the beginning. Liebling, what do I do here?" he asked, but he was not talking to Lance. The Tiger waited as the old Witch pleaded with his departed wife for guidance.

"Uncle Uzzi?" he said after some minutes of silence had passed.

"I've told you all a million times. The women Fate chooses for you are to be cherished. They are smart, sassy, and deserve to know the truth up front. *Honesty*, you big fur ball, is always the best policy."

"I know, Uncle Uzzi," Lance grumbled, voice still cracking with emotion as he spoke. He was too distraught to care if that telltale sign gave anything away. "Annalia is my fated mate. I will do anything to make her happy."

"I know you mean that Lance, and that's why I will say this. There is a luncheon reveal for Graves Enterprises new video game release. *Fire Battles* is being unveiled at the Villa in *Maccon City*. That's why she came here, you know, to work on the sequel. She wanted to experience, and study snow in real life," the Witch explained. "Are you writing this down?"

"Yes, sir," Lance grabbed a pencil and paper.

"That's the Villa Ristorante, the one on Route 35. She was going to skip it, but after last night she needed some space."

"If she needs space, why are you telling me this?"

"Because someone cleaned out her apartment and is tracking her down as we speak."

"What?" he roared.

"Easy! My ears are sensitive too, you big hairball," Uncle Uzzi huffed out a breath. "I suspect it's her sister and her husband, Anna's brother-in-law. She's told you about them, right?"

"Yes," he hissed angrily.

From what he knew, Annalia's sister and her husband were more interested in putting down his sexy, sweet mate than in helping her.

Hell no.

They probably had some scheme to get her to go back to Florida with them. He might only have known her for a short while, but he needed her like he needed air. There was no way he was going to go home and mope while Anna's sister and husband told her how to live her life. That was so not happening on his watch

"Then you better get a move on," Uncle Uzzi said, and for some reason he knew the man was smiling. "Curtain goes up in ninety minutes."

Lance knew better than to dally. Hauling ass to the shower, he went over the things he was going to say to his mate when he saw her. He was sorrier than he could ever apologize for. He'd fucked this thing up from the beginning, but he needed her to know last night was not a one-night stand.

Truth was he'd been burning with desire for her from the second he'd scented her through the door. Every fiber of his being, his animal included, knew she was his.

Anna looked so beautiful all dressed up, even better naked mused. What was it she'd said when they were dancing?

Magic.

And she was right, Being with her was like magic. But even that had nothing on the way he felt about her. She was his true and fated mate. Annalia was the one being in the whole universe who could tame his Tiger's soul.

He'd claimed her with his bite, and even now felt their bond calling him to her. Lance jumped out of the shower, ignoring the pounding on the door until he could grab a towel.

"Open up," the command came from the one person in the world who could make him veer off course.

The fucking Neta with his Alpha voice. He didn't have time for this, but he could not afford to piss off the leader of the Maverick Pride. Not when he intended to bring his very human mate into the fold. Still, Lance's Tiger growled while he tightened his towel, and stalked towards the door.

"Hunter, I—"

Lance stopped talking as he got a good look at his Pride leader. What the fuck was the Neta wearing?

Lance blinked twice at the man who had one tiny precious bundle strapped to what looked like some kind of reverse backpack covered in pink bows to his chest, and the other chubby cherub was in a similar pack high up on his back, covered in pink and black tiger stripes.

That one was way better, in Lance's opinion. His Neta's usually recognizable shaved head was covered by a neon yellow snow cap. Obviously his mate's doing.

Lance stifled his laughter, but he wasn't fooling anyone. Hunter just glared at his guard. It was hard to take him seriously with his baby girls cooing and giggling with delight. One was drooling on said skullcap, and the other was kicking her booted feet into her father's abdomen. They'd obviously been on some kind of family romp through the woods.

Lance knew it was a family walk, because a moment later he was shoved aside by a small blonde whirlwind. The Nari was in his cabin, and she was seething.

"Where is she? You are in so much trouble." Elissa

reached into her pocket and pulled out a water pistol, which she then emptied in Lance's face. "Bad kitty!"

"Baaaaddd!" squealed Melly.

"Kiiitttyyyyyyyy!" Celia was next.

Traitorous munchkins. Lance mock-frowned at them and they giggled some more.

"Okay, enough of that," Hunter grumbled and took the gun from his wife, who was still searching the cabin. "Where is the human?"

"Neta, with all due respect, she is my mate—"

"Ha! As if that matters," Elissa squeaked. "There are rules, buddy. You can't just go around biting people without consequences," she growled and finally stopped long enough to look at the younger Tiger.

"Well, at least you showed her a good time. Right? Am I right? I mean cause, Lance, I always thought of you as way too young for me, but I have to say, you look old enough to—what?" Elissa turned and rolled her eyes at her husband who was openly snarling to his twins' delight.

Lance frowned, squirming under his Nari's gaze. Shit. Hunter's skin was peppered with the orange and black fur of his beast the second he caught on to his wife's perusal of his guard's body. Once again, Lance was almost compelled to drop to his knees.

"Please, Neta," he said. "Allow me to put on some clothes, and I will tell you both everything."

"Honey, stop growling." She put her hand on Hunter's arm. "You know you are the only pussy for me," she whispered, not nearly low enough, but the Neta stilled, and Lance took the opportunity to grab some clothes.

Thank fuck.

He really didn't want Elissa ogling him—as in ever. That would be like his older sister getting an eyeful.

Gross.

Even more compelling, he did not want Hunter to rip his fucking head off. The Neta was fiercely possessive of his mate. Something Lance could only recently relate to. Either way, he wasn't into strutting with his junk out in front of the Nari. And of course, then there were the twins to think of.

Eeeek!

Even his Tiger couldn't allow that scenario to play out. Hunter would kill him for sure. Nudity was common around Shifters, but that was between shifting. Not just for the hell of it.

Lance and his Tiger both agreed. There was only

one woman he wanted to witness his nudity. His mate—only, Anna had run out on him before he had the chance to explain what his bite meant.

Shit.

"Spill," the Nari commanded from behind the door.

Lance frowned as he tugged on his pants and socks, but he did as he was asked. Lance told the ruling couple of the Maverick Pride everything. Every. Single. Detail.

Well, except the X-rated ones. Those were personal and to be shared with one person only. His Annalia. Lance would get her back. He simply had to.

"Really, not sharing any of the good parts?"

Lance heard the frown in Elissa's voice and he rolled his eyes.

"I saw that," she growled.

"How?" he asked, bewildered by her scary Nari-ness.

"Just hurry already."

"Damn," he growled, tugging on his boots. "I'm going to be late. My car is still at the event from last night."

Lance cursed himself for being a fool. He had no car, no girl, and the ruling couple of the Maverick

Pride had come to his cabin on foot. He was beside himself. Taking a deep breath, he rested his elbows on his knees, and placed his hands on his head.

Staring at the area rug where he'd knelt and worshiped his mate's sweet body last night. Fuck. How could things have gone so wrong, so fast? Then he saw it. Annalia's inhaler. It must have tumbled from her purse last night.

Oh no.

What if she needed it? What if she had an asthma attack?

Shit!

He had to get it to her. He could Shift, and Elissa could tie a bag with his clothes around his neck. Yes, that could work.

"Nari," he said, and opened the door. "Can you help me? I'm going to—"

"Go outside and get the keys from Brayden?" she supplied with a knowing smirk.

"What?"

"He's pulling up now, Lance," Hunter explained and walked over to him, sans baby slings. The Neta clapped a meaty hand on his shoulder.

"What you did was dumb as fuck," Hunter growled. "But we all make mistakes. Now, go make it up to her."

"Look at him, Hunter. Our baby guard is all grown up and getting himself mated," Elissa mumbled. She wiped a tear from her eye as the babies played on the carpet.

"Uh, are you okay?" Lance asked before he left.

"Yeah, I'm good. Remember to sweep her off her feet. And, for f—*fudge's sake*, talk to the woman. Leave the *bowchickawowow* for after the words," Elissa said and smiled at her mate who *tsked* his wife.

Their combined efforts to not curse around the two precious cubs were hardly working, but they were still the best people Lance knew. They were his Pride. They were his family. And that meant everything.

But he knew he would leave Maverick Point if Anna wanted him to go. Heartbreaking as the thought was, he would do anything for Annalia. She was his entire world now. Nothing else mattered, except bringing his mate back home. And to him, home was where she was.

Hunter would understand. Lance nodded his farewells before running outside to where Brayden had just parked one of the Maverick Development SUVs.

"Hear you have a mate to track down," the enormous Black Bear Shifter grunted.

"Yeah, I do," Lance agreed. "What if I fuck it up?"

"You will, about a hundred different times," Brayden said and grinned. "But don't worry, man, making up is half the fun."

He hoped like fuck that Brayden was right.

Grrrrrr.

Chapter Thirteen

L ance nodded at the Bear and climbed inside the vehicle. The Beta closed the driver's door, and Lance gunned it down the highway. About ten minutes out, he got pulled over, and received a speeding ticket for his efforts. The seaside town of Maccon City was about an hour away and run by the Macconwood Pack, Wolf Shifters the lot of them

The cop insisted on a license check, which was simply more bad luck. His Tiger was growling even more now, so Lance did something he never thought he would do. He called the Macconwood Pack house, and they got in a call to Cat Maccon-Nighthawk of the Sheriff's department.

He explained to the officer that pulled him over

that his wife had forgotten her asthma pump, but the cop was being a hard ass. It wasn't until the Werewolf named Cat had put in a call that the officer had let him go with a handful of tickets and a warning to mind the law.

Lance thanked him anyway, took the tickets, and even pledged to send a large donation to the Policemen's Ball the next time around. Once he entered the city limits, finding the Villa was easy.

It was a large banquet hall that had been rented out for the Graves Enterprises unveiling event. Anna had mentioned working for Randall Graves, a member of the local Wolf Pack, if memory served him right. The guy was a software genius, and the founder of many popular video games.

Lance parked the truck and jumped out, booted feet crunching the snow as he did. He could not scent her with all the different smells in the air, and one long look had his Tiger was going nuts.

Shit.

There had to be a thousand people there. Maybe more. As he moved inside, he saw it was set up like any other convention. At least two-hundred booths and half as many stands were arranged in rows selling or demonstrating new advancements in gaming tech and graphic art.

At the center of it all was a small dais and podium. He recognized a few members of the neighboring Barvale Clan, as well as some of the Macconwood Pack Wolves milling about. Lance nodded politely, but he was scanning the crowds for one person only.

Finally, his Tiger breathed in deeply. Every single cell in his body tensed. His stomach did somersaults, and his heart went crazy off the rails like a runaway train. The familiar scent of chocolate, cherries, and chili pepper mixed with just a hint of Tiger reached his nostrils.

It was only moments then till Lance located her with unerring accuracy. Need raced through his veins, desire spiking his blood. It made it difficult to think, but that was natural. He'd already claimed the gorgeous female, and though new, their matebond was already strong.

She was too good for him. He knew it, and yet, he could not let go. Everything he knew about her solidified his belief that she was one in a million—a gem among the gravel.

The Graves Enterprises *Battles* series were the best games on the market, and as he neared her, his eyes glanced at the huge banner that listed the designers and developers. Her name was credited on all six of the games.

His sweet Anna had been modest when she said she made a pretty good loving. She was a brilliant graphic designer, and responsible for some of the best levels on those games. Being an avid player, Lance recognized skill when he saw it. She was so smart and talented.

Too good for me.

No. She is purrfect, his beast growled.

he stood like a deer in headlights. *Fuck.* What if she rejected him? What if she turned him away? Lance had no doubt his Tiger would go insane almost immediately. The animal needed her almost as much as the man did. It was worth the risk. He knew that without a doubt. Anna coughed, and Lance was on the move.

Sweet mate needs us, the Tiger chuffed.

Yes, he agreed.

He just had to prove he could be everything she'd ever want and more. And he would, happily too, for the rest of their lives.

"Annalia," he called out, his voice hoarser than he would have liked.

"Lance? What are you doing here?" Anna asked and blinked at him curiously.

"You were gone," he began.

"I know, I left a note," she said, but he shook his head.

"No, no note."

"It was taped to the front door. Didn't you see it? I'm sorry, Lance," she whispered, and pulled him over to where they would have less of an audience.

"Why did you go?"

"I just didn't want to be there when you woke up and asked me to leave," she explained and bit her lip.

"What? Why would I ever want you to leave, Anna? I claimed you last night."

"Claimed me?"

"I thought you understood," he growled and ran a hand through his hair. He was still fucking this up. She was gonna kill him.

"Understood what?"

"I told you I wanted to make you mine. You said yes. I claimed you with my bite, Anna. Marked you as mine."

"What does that mean?" she whispered the question, brown eyes glued to his.

"Anna," he whispered, afraid to lose her. "It means my Tiger chooses you. I choose you to be mine."

"Oh," she whispered, eyes wide. "I just thought all that growly mine stuff meant you liked me a little."

"Liked you? Honey, I love you," he told her, eyes

on hers. "I know it seems impossible and fast, but that is how it is for Shifters. I love you, Anna. You are my mate. My beast knew it the moment I breathed in your scent."

"I have a confession," she said. "I called Uncle Uzzi this morning and he explained a little to me. You see, my parents always told me and my sister it was love at first sight for them. Sandra thought it was dumb, but I never did. From the second I saw you lance, I knew too. I love you," she told him, and his heart soared.

Lance moved to kiss her but she stopped him with one hand raised. Fuck. What was wrong? She looked sad and nervous, so he waited for her to find the words she needed. Giving her space was diffi-cult, but he would always give her what she needed. Even if it killed him.

This is what he rushed here for, right? To tell her what she meant to him. He probably should have played out some scenarios in his head where she told him to fuck off.

"Okay, first, I have to ask you something, Lance."

"Okay."

"Are you really twenty-six?"

"I wasn't expecting that question, but yeah. I am. Why?"

"Well, I'm already thirty. Maybe you want to reconsider this whole mating thing."

"Shifters don't care about age, love," he explained and smiled gently. "It would not matter if you were thirty or three hundred, I would still choose you. I want you, Anna. All of you."

"You do?" Disbelief swam in her eyes. "But you hardly know me."

"I know everything I need to know to pick you, sweet. Everything else we can learn together. If you would just give me a chance to prove it to you," he whispered.

Please, he begged in his mind, *please give me a chance.*

Those deep brown globes were bright and beautiful under a curtain of wildly curly hair. And Lance stilled.

Wait. What?

"Your hair is curly," he grinned.

"Oh, yeah." Anna straightened her shoulders as if daring him to say something. "It frizzes all the time. Yesterday, I had to sit in that salon chair for an hour and a half to get it to look like that. And it's not something I do very often. Also, the clothes, I don't dress like that a lot as you can see," she said and pointed to her leggings and sweater.

"Anna, not that you didn't look gorgeous last night, because you did," he said and stalked closer. "But I have never seen a woman look as hot as you do right now."

"I look hot in leggings with my hair sticking up?"

"Fuck yeah. Like a sexy little nerd girl with a smoking body and a killer grin. Anna, you are the most gorgeous woman I have ever seen."

As if to prove it, Lance grabbed her in his arms, pulling her against the hard evidence of his ever ready arousal. He nuzzled her neck, loving the way she fit inside his embrace and sighed into him.

"Oh," she replied and swallowed.

"Can I touch your hair?" Lance asked, reaching up tentatively, noting her tension.

Some women hated to have their hair touched, but he couldn't help himself. He needed to get his hands on the wealth of hair atop her head. Like a crown, he mused.

The corkscrew curls were held together by a simple black band on top of her head. He could not stop grinning, imagining them spread across his pillow. They were so awesome, tumbling down like curly ribbon or spiral pasta.

He sounded like a fucking idiot, but what did he know? He wasn't a poet. Still, Lance knew pretty, and that was her. All her. His Annalia with the incredible hair.

"Your hair is gorgeous," he said and touched the tendrils carefully testing its softness after she nodded her assent.

He cupped her face, kissing her head, then her nose, and finally her lips.

"I love you, my beautiful mate."

Everything that had gone wrong the last few hours seemed to slip away under the warm, steady pressure of his mouth on hers. She was in his arms, and she was allowing him to kiss her. Hell, she was kissing him back.

Anna's ready acceptance and submission was his undoing. He deepened the kiss, tasting the apple she must've just eaten along with her own spicy chocolate sweetness. She was perfection itself as she sighed and leaned into him with her luscious body.

Christ, he loved this woman. More than anything. He ached for her, his cock throbbed, body trembled, and Lance could hardly catch his breath as their kiss slowed.

He pressed his forehead to hers, and she rubbed his shoulders and nuzzled his neck. Soothing him, calming the beast like no other. He never wanted to let her go. He would do anything to keep her right there where she belonged.

"Annalia? You're on," a young man with a microphone interrupted her.

He turned his head and growled at the young punk. How dare he interrupt when he was holding his woman?

Grrrr.

But Anna was pushing out of his arms, and albeit reluctantly, Lance had to let her go.

"What? Oh damn,." She looked at him then at Lance, indecision in her eyes. "It's my job, I have to go and talk to the crowd—" Her cheeks were bright pink, and he smiled, realizing she wasn't leaving forever. Just for a moment.

"Go on," Lance said. "I'll be waiting. Oh, here. In case you need it."

He handed her the pump, and some of his speeding tickets.

"Whoops, those are mine," he mumbled and scratched the back of his neck with embarrassment.

"You got a ticket trying to bring me my pump?" Anna asked and smiled at him.

It was like the sun shining down on him and him alone, basking him in its warmth, even though he knew damn well it was eighteen degrees outside.

Anna was his own personal sun, and his world revolved around her. Always would.

As it should, he thought.

Mate, chuffed his beast happily.

Anna blew him away with that smile.

"Annalia," he breathed her name, taking her in with his eyes.

"You'll wait?" she asked, deep brown eyes boring into him.

"Always."

Of course, he would wait.

"Then we'll finish talking," she repeated.

Lance wondered what he'd done to deserve such a beautiful, honest, and deliciously sweet mate. Yes, they would talk. And hopefully more.

"Yes, love, I am not going anywhere without you," he vowed.

"Okay," she said and took the microphone from the increasingly anxious convention worker and approached the dais.

"Everyone," a tall man with long hair and a beard, Lance recognized at once as Randall Graves, owner of Graves Enterprises.

"It is my privilege to announce one of our most talented design artists. A woman whose work allowed *Fire Battles* to take the gamer into an entirely different world all together, Ms. Annalia Reese."

An uproarious applause welcomed his mate onto the stage, and pride shot through him. He whistled and clapped with the rest of them, noting with joy the faint blush along her cheeks.

Lance was mesmerized. When she spoke, Anna showed humility and gratitude, downplaying her role in the other *Battles* video games that he himself had spent many an hour playing. But it didn't matter, the fans knew his mate, and they loved her.

An hour of her speaking then answering questions from the crowd flew by, but Lance was so enraptured by her sincerity, and of course, her adorable bashfulness, he could not tear his eyes away. Her curls bounced whenever she laughed or shrugged, shooting his mind straight to the gutter.

He couldn't wait to see them bouncing with her on top of him. Just picturing her riding him was making him so hard, he damn near burst through his pants.

But once he got started, he couldn't stop thinking about it. He wanted her. Always would.

Lance had made some mistakes, like not explaining what his bite meant. But it was done now, and Lance refused to let go. She belonged with him, and he most assuredly belonged to her. His Tiger would have no other.

Before he'd left his cabin, Hunter had cornered him. The Neta asked him a few questions Lance had never considered. As he watched her onstage explaining the process that went into creating the various levels of heat and flame, the hours of study and trial and error necessary to recreate the effects in the video game, Lance replayed Hunter's words in his mind.

"Have you thought what she might think about you? The fooling around, the not taking anything seriously. You have a reputation for being a clown, Lance. It's true, but I know there is more inside of you. Having a mate changes a man. Are you willing to give all that nonsense up for her? If you aren't, don't get in that car. Stay right here. We will find a way to break the mating mark."

"With all due respect, Neta, no fucking way. She is mine. Nothing matters without her."

It was true. Every word he'd said. She was the most important thing in his world. Yes, he'd been an ass to some mated members of his Pride, and he imagined everyone in Maverick Point would be taking shots at him for a good long while, but he deserved it.

He would take it all in stride as long as she stayed

with him. As long as his Anna forgave him and remained by his side. As long as she allowed him to endeavor to deserve her.

It would probably take eighty years or so, but damn it would be fun trying.

Mine.

Chapter Fourteen

Lance watched her with covetous eyes as Anna shook hands with Randall Graves once more before leaving the dais. He headed over to the small staircase, anxious to finish their chat, but before he reached her, she was waylaid.

A slightly older woman with one of those angry haircuts where the pieces stuck up in the back was speaking in a low, sharp voice. A middle-aged man with a noticeable paunch stood beside her, his face a mirror image of her own, The man was nodding his head in agreement with whatever that woman was saying, and when Lance looked at his mate, he noted Anna was not happy.

"Sandra? What are you doing here?"

Lance was finally close enough to hear what was being said over the din of the surrounding crowd. His mate gasped when the woman grabbed her arm and began to tug.

"Anna?" he called.

Anna's gaze flicked over to him, and she dug her heels in.

Good girl.

Lance's Tiger was snarling in fury at the woman's hand. He reined in the beast, but it was not easy.

"What is going on here?" he growled and approached.

"Thank you for having my back," She told him then turned to face the two stunned adults. "But I got this, Lance."

"Lance? Who the hell is this guy, Annie? He is obviously using you. Look at me," the woman said and snapped her fingers in Anna's face.

Anna squared her shoulders, looking like an angry little spitfire. She growled too, like a total badass and held the woman's gaze.

"Sandra, enough! First, my name is Annalia, or Anna. Not Annie. Never Annie." Annalia hissed. She pulled back against her sister's hold.

The older woman turned around, expelling an

annoyed breath that did not even move her overly hair-sprayed bangs.

"Ugh, it doesn't even matter, Annie. I told you, we need you to come home. Now, let's go," she scolded.

"Sandra, Glenn, this is Lance. He's my boyfriend. Lance this is my sister and her husband," Annalia explained and Lance's chest puffed up.

All his protective instincts on high alert. Still, he was gratified to see his presence soothed her obviously frayed nerves as she pressed close to his side. Whatever these two wanted, it was obviously not what she wanted.

"Boyfriend? Really, Annie," her sister scoffed. "We are your family. Let's just go already."

"Yes. This is none of your business, buddy," Glenn said, addressing Lance.

"Like Anna said, I am with her. So, if this concerns her, it is very much my business," he told the man and allowed a hint of his Tiger to lace his words.

"You can't just butt in on stuff that has nothing to do with you, buddy—"

"I stay until she says go, understand?"

"OMG! Are you threatening us? Annie! He is threatening us.

"I am not threatening anyone, lady. It's merely a promise."

Grrrrrrr.

Chapter Fifteen

"Alright, everyone needs to calm down," Anna pressed her side into Lance.

The feel of his big warm body near her made her resolve that much firmer. Sandra was always running roughshod over Anna, but not this time.

She couldn't believe this was happening. Why was her sister even here? And Glenn? Since when did he even acknowledge Anna?

"This is family business," Sandra said in that same bored, annoyed voice that always grated on Annalia's nerves.

"Well, good," Anna said and put her hand in Lance's, ridiculously glad when he squeezed tightly. "He's my family too."

"What?" Glenn barked.

"Oh no, you do not get to say that after knowing him for what? Half a day! Jesus Christ, you can't go falling for the first guy to pay you a little attention, Annie!" Sandra screeched.

"Sandra, don't you want me to be happy? Mom and Dad always talked about love at first sight, and I found that too. Why can't you just accept it?" Anna asked her sister, eyes big and round, begging her to understand.

She looked so sad and earnest, Lance's heart squeezed. His mate was so beautiful and kind-hearted, and her sister was just so damn cruel, determined to beat her down.

Fuck that. Not on his watch. He stood right behind his Anna, a steady hand on her lower back. This was not his fight, and he needed to allow her to take point. But she should know he was right there if she needed him to step in. He had her back and always would.

"Annie, no more nonsense. You need to come home with us. You haven't even looked at the quarterly documents, much less signed them," Sandra said and sniffed.

"You can't even do the simple things we have asked of you. How many times did I tell you? Those documents are important. You can't live up here on your own when you forget your obligations to your family. Now, you are coming back home," Glenn whisper yelled. His voice was pinched and made the hair on the back of Lance's neck stand up. he might not want to butt in on the sister when she spoke, but this male had best get the fuck away from his mate.

"Back off, Glenn," Lance growled in a muffled voice.

The man looked like he was going to burst that vein in his forehead if he didn't calm down.

"It's fine," Anna told him. "Glenn always was dramatic, right Glenn? And I don't know if you or my sister noticed, but I am not your ward any longer. I am not a child. I do not need your permission to live where I want to live."

"You spoiled brat. Have you no idea—"

"Glenn, I would be really careful right now," Lance interrupted.

Annalia's heart was racing. This was beyond embarrassing, but here it was. The confrontation she had been dodging with her family for years now. Lance stood behind her, safe, warm, secure. She felt protected and loved with him in her corner, and damn, if she hadn't already fallen for him hard, she would have right then.

Glenn was spitting mad, spouting hateful things at her. Anna was shocked. She had never seen him lose it like that. Lance uttered a warning, but she feared her brother-in-law was too dense to hear the growl in Lance's voice. From what she had read in her fiction books about Shifters, they were possessive and old-fashioned in their treatment of women, especially their mates. Lance would not like her brother-in-law's snipey attitude with her.

"Sandra? Are you going to let Glenn talk to me like that?" Anna looked to her sister for aid, but Sandra just nodded, agreeing with her husband.

Her red-nailed hands dug into her too skinny hips, and Annalia noted how unhealthy she looked. Like plastic.

The sweet sister she'd loved when she was a baby didn't exist anymore. She hadn't for a long time.

Sandra was different now. All edges and planes. She was Botox and war paint. There was nothing left underneath all that armor. Years of caring about money and keeping up with the Joneses had killed all her warmth. She didn't know what love was. She certainly had none for her little sister.

"Did you ever love me?" Anna asked.

"What? Anna don't be stupid. I took you in. Glenn did. We didn't send you to foster care when we could have."

"Hmm, you mean when we *should* have," her husband added.

Pain gripped Annalia's heart, followed by the rolling growl coming from Lance. His presence soothed her, but this was going to hurt no matter what. She'd hoped they cared even a little about her, about her happiness. But with those careless words, Sandra, and Glenn had destroyed every dream of family she'd ever had when she'd lived with them.

Just like they had with everything else she had tried to salvage after her parents had died. Like when she had dreamed of finding her true love, and they'd told her not to bother. What sad little people they were.

"True love is for princesses, Anna, not chubby little girls." Sandra's angry voice played in her mind.

"You know something, Sandra, I don't think you ever loved me," Anna confessed sadly.

"What? Have you have lost your mind! Thinking of you with this stranger making you think all these lies just makes me sick, Annie. It's a good thing I packed your apartment up," Sandra grabbed a cigarette from her pocket and lit. "We are going now."

Annalia covered her mouth and nose and backed up a step. Her sister always smoked around her, uncaring of the fact it triggered many of her allergies and led to a severe difficulty in breathing.

"Put that out," Lance growled, but Sandra just laughed.

"As if I would listen to you. What are you? Some money hungry gigolo, think my sister is loaded or something? It's the only way a guy like you would want her fat ass," Sandra said and looked him up and down.

Anna ignored the sting of her sister's words and grabbed Lance's arm when he would have defended her. He was sweet, but she needed to handle this.

"Fat jokes all you got, Sandra? You never were very imaginative," she told her meaner, older sister. "Are you serious about emptying my apartment? You had no right."

Anna glared at her sibling. She'd been pushed too far this time. Sandra might be her older sister, but Annalia had paid her debt long ago. These people did not have an affectionate bone in their bodies.

They just stood and glared scathingly at her. Like she was dirt.

"Look, you owe us, *pudge-bear*," her sister said, trying for playful by using the nickname she'd called her as a kid, which Anna hated by the way. "We paid for college and your first car—"

"You gave me your old car, and I had to have the engine and transmission rebuilt. And I paid you back almost in full now for college. You know what here," she looked in her purse and pulled out the envelope she had addressed to them, thrusting it at the sister she barely recognized.

"This is the last payment I owe you for my college loan. Don't worry Glenn, I included the bank interest like I always do! Now, I want both of you to leave me alone. And don't ever come back here."

"W-what about, Rory?" Sandra asked.

Her sister looked doubtful for the first time in Annalia's memory. She wondered why, but it was too little too late.

"My nephew can come see me anytime he likes," she answered.

The little boy spent most of his life with nannies and tutors. Thank goodness. The result was that he was smart and sensitive. Nothing at all like his parents.

"Look, Annalia, let's discuss this privately," Glenn tried.

"No," she said, grateful again for Lance's strong and steady presence.

The big man's warmth seeped through her clothes, chasing away the sudden chill Sandra and Glenn brought with them. There was something about the way he stood just there, behind her. Powerful, but quiet. Allowing her to take the lead, but ready to jump in should she need him. He seemed content to let her take care of things, and she loved him even more for that vote of confidence.

Anna had expected a more overbearing display of machismo. Something she didn't think she could handle. This was her mess, and she needed to clean it up. Luckily for her, her mate gave her just what she needed.

"There is nothing else to say. Except goodbye," she turned and looked up into Lance's beautiful, clear eyes.

"I am going to live my life how I want, and that's with you."

She never thought blue could be so hot, and yet there was fire in his unwavering gaze. It was like nothing she'd ever seen. So much heat and desire, and if she wasn't mistaken, affection too.

Burning blue lava rocks, the kind people placed in outdoor fire pits.

That was what his eyes reminded her of, and they pulled her in like a crystalline magnet. She smiled widely. Noting at first the shock, then the gratitude as he dipped down to brush his lips against hers.

"Should we go talk now?" she asked.

"Yeah," Lance said. "I'd like that."

"Wait!" Sandra interrupted them, pulling a snarl from the big man holding her.

Annalia grinned and patted his chest. Turning round, she faced her sister.

"What is it?"

"Well, you see. Annie, *er*, Anna, the truth is, I lied," she gasped. "All those years ago when mother and father died, they didn't leave us nothing. Daddy didn't lose it all."

"What?" Anna gasped. She'd never fully understood how her father, who'd been a successful real estate mogul could have lost his entire estate just before he and his wife died in a horrible car accident.

"The money, the house, everything they had was to be split evenly between the two of us. You were just a baby though. Still in school, and I was already out of high school. *I* had to take care of *you*. It wasn't fair," she sniffed.

"Wait, what? You always told me I had nothing. That you and Glenn gave me everything I had," she said, disbelief ringing in her voice. "You made me write down everything I ever spent. You kept a running tally my whole life and made me pay it back."

"You stole from your sister," Lance echoed, sympathy for Anna, and anger at them filled his voice.

He was right. That was exactly what she did. Sandra and Glenn had stolen from her. Not just money, but her peace of mind. They'd done it for years. Horror and pain squeezed Anna's chest.

"All those years, you were so mean to me," she whispered aloud. "Told me I was too fat to find a man. Told me my job was unimportant and trivial. Said my art was nothing. I believed you. I thought I was worthless. I turned myself inside out trying to please you."

Anger infused Annalia's voice as she faced off with the one person who should have always loved and protected her. Sandra was her family. This kind of betrayal was beyond her scope of understanding.

Only Lance's steady presence made it bearable.

She sucked in a breath despite the tightening of her lungs. An unfortunate side effect whenever she became too angry.

She felt something being pushed in her palm and looked to see Lance had handed her the pump. Annalia nodded and took two puffs before answering her sister.

Sweat had started to bead on her forehead, and her stomach clutched in anger. She was positively nauseous. But Anna was far too angry to let this go.

"You lied to me. Stole from me. And made me feel like shit for the last time," she told Sandra.

The pain was making her double over. Anna was sweating now. The pump was not helping, but thankfully, at some point, Lance had led them all to a small, private room so they were not being watched by an audience.

"Anna?" he asked, crouching next to her.

"I'm fine. But you two, I don't want to see either of you again. At least not for a good, long while. I will have my lawyer in touch with yours, but you better get all the documents you have regarding my half of the inheritance from our parents," she instructed them.

In all honesty, Anna did not care about the money, but this was her legacy from her parents.

Sandra and Glenn had tried to rob her of that. They needed to make amends.

"You can't do that. We have nothing left. We've been living off your half for years—"

"Then I suggest you both get real jobs and figure out how you are going to move forward paying me back. And Sandra, have my things returned to the condo immediately. You can keep that check to get back home," Anna told her sister coolly though she felt crippling pain inside. Something was wrong, but she was not about to show weakness to either of them.

"But wait," her sister said. "That's it? You're going to just leave with that strange man?"

"He isn't that strange," she replied, and looked at Lance, her heart in her eyes. He smirked, kissing her hand, narrowing his eyes when she winced as another wave of cramps hit her.

"But yes, Sandra, I'm going to build a life with this man. It might sound ridiculous to you. I mean, we only just met, but I feel better about myself when I am with him than I ever had in an entire lifetime of being near you."

"That's a terrible thing to say," Sandra whimpered, Glenn patting her shoulder awkwardly.

"Is it? Then I suggest you leave before I really

start sharing," Anna growled, eyes widening at the feral sound.

Lance turned his head and glared at the pair of them, and Annalia stifled the nervous laugh that bubbled up inside as they ran out the door. She allowed Lance to take her hand and lift her in his arms.

"What are you doing?" she asked, whimpering as another wave of cramps hit her.

"Come on. Gotta get you out of here," he growled.

She was about two seconds from hyperventilating. The pressure of his arms around her felt good as he carried her outside through the quickly increasing snowfall to his SUV. For some reason, she didn't even feel the chill. In fact, she felt warm.

Like really, really warm.

Grrrr.

Chapter Sixteen

"I don't know what's wrong with me," Anna grunted and tried breathing, but the pain in her stomach was too strong. "I don't, I don't feel well."

"Shit. Anna? Can you hear me?"

She could, but there was no room to answer. Her brain was being bombarded with so many emotions.

Anger at her sister. Desire for her mate. Eagerness to run in the snow and play like a wild thing.

It was like something inside of her was biting and scratching against her skin. The tearing and burning sensations were growing. Her nerve-endings screamed as the feelings intensified. Her gums ached, *hell*, even her nailbeds hurt.

"What is happening?" she looked down and screeched.

"Oh fuck," Lance growled, eyes wide.

Her usually short fingernails now resembled three-inch-long, black claws, orange and black fur began to sprout out along her skin. Something inside of her was pissed. It wanted to hunt her sister down and smack the bitch for what she'd done. The animalistic instinct seemed to intensify, as did the pain.

"It's the *Puspa*," growled Lance. "Baby, are you okay? Fuck, I didn't know. I'm so sorry. Listen to me, my love. I gave you my claiming bite, but the Fates blessed us even further."

"Blessed us? This hurts like fuck, Lance."

She knew instinctively that extra *grrrr* in his voice was his beast. When he glanced at her, she saw the animal in his eyes. Worry and concern, along with other, deeper emotions flooded her.

It was almost overwhelming, but that pain she felt still held her in its grips. It wouldn't allow her to be swept away by the tide of emotions that was her mate's own feelings.

Mine.

What the? A voice inside her seemed to be calling out. It wanted to claim him. To mark him.

Mine. Yes, mine.

"Shit, Annalia, you must listen to me," Lance cursed and slammed the steering wheel with his hands. "This is too fast, but Uncle Uzzi explained you were my mate, right? Last night, when we made love, and I bit you, that was my animal side claiming you as mate. In doing so, I sealed our *matebond,* accepting the universe's blessing, that's you, essentially. Shifters know their mates. You are mine. But my bite did something else—"

"What the fuck did it do? Ow!" she roared, like really fucking roared in pain.

The highway was only semi-crowded, a good thing for the Garden State Parkway. The snow was coming down faster, but the roads were salted and clear for now. Lance pressed the gas pedal hard.

"Aghhhhhh. Laannncccceeeee!" She tossed her head from side to side. It was too much.

"I gave you a Tiger," he whispered. "Easy, love, hold on a few minutes more," he cajoled, but it was no good.

Whatever was happening, it was happening now. She heard the metal in the seat bend as she pushed back against the passenger side chair.

Fucking hell, she was breaking his car.

"I don't give a shit about the car," he grunted. "Fuck, baby, I am so sorry I did not even think about this as a possibility because it is so rare. Don't fight her, Anna. Let your she-Cat in. She won't hurt you anymore than she has to."

His fingers gripped the steering wheel so hard his knuckles were white with the strain. Then she knew. Deep inside, she understood they were connected.

Lance was right there with her, feeling her pain, going through whatever this was that held her tight in its relentless grip.

"*Puspa*," he told her the strange word again, and she waited for him to continue. "It means *awakening* in Bengali. I awakened the beast within you, love. Let her in, Anna."

"I'm a Shifter now? Lance," she growled his name in disbelief.

Roooooooooooaaaaaaaaaaarrrrrrrrrr.

Yes, that sound was her. She was growling at him. Like a fucking Tiger.

"Sandra made you mad. Tiger wants to protect."

He was reduced to barely understandable sentence fragments. But she knew exactly what he was saying. It all rang true. Deep in that place inside her, Anna felt her animal spirit trying desperately to make contact, to connect. All she had to do was let her.

She'd been through so much with Lance in such a short time. Who would believe all this could happen in only a couple of days? But it was happening regardless of belief.

Anna had mistakenly trusted her sister and Glenn to do what was best for her when she'd been growing up, and that was a mistake.

It was her turn now to decide. From the photo albums and her mother's diary, she knew her parents had shared an intense love. Her mother claimed she'd fallen for her man at first sight, and Anna had always dreamed of the same thing happening to her.

This was her shot. With Lance she wasn't risking her heart, she was letting it soar. People might think it was crazy, but who cared what people think anyway? Not Anna. She was going to hold on to Lance with both hands, *er*, claws.

Mine!

With a tremendous roar and a bone-breaking crunch, Anna let it happen. Lance threw the SUV in park and jumped out of the car to open her door. Not a second too soon, either. Tigers were big as fuck. And heavy, too.

"Come on, baby," he stood back, crooning to her in his deep, sexy baritone.

Annalia leapt from the ruined vehicle. She sniffed and chuffed at the falling snow. A million different stimuli invaded her heightened senses, but Lance was there to walk her through it.

He whispered encouragingly, praising her beauty and strength. Anna had to admit her feline side was so on board with that. Everyone liked to be complimented now and then. Even pussies.

Rrrroooaaaaarrr!

"Damn, you are so beautiful," he said and grinned widely and sank to the floor despite the gathering snow.

Annalia chuffed again, feeling his pride in her as if it were her own. Growling, she bumped his chest with her large, feline head. She could hardly believe it. Anna was a Tiger—a real, honest to gods, striped fur having, tail swaying, fangs dripping, huge snarly ass Tiger.

"She-Tiger, love."

Her mate was still grinning at her, and she wanted to shake him. Panic flared to life. How could he do this to her? Why didn't he tell her? But just as quickly, she let all that go. Besides, he was too cute to ruin with her new claws.

Still, he deserved a little displeasure, so she hissed and snarled, snapping her jaws as close to his face as she dared get. Then she pushed him with her massive head once again, and he rolled over laughing.

The jerk.

"Let me shift, love. Then we can run together," he said, and his invitation was made with a low rumble that made even her furry bits quake with need.

Fuck.

In her fur, she recognized him as her fated mate down to her soul. All the doubts her human side had with trying to reconcile her fantasy of love at first sight, was nothing compared to the reality that was her feelings for Lance.

The wintergreen scent she'd thought was simply a breath mint he'd eaten last night invaded her nostrils, and she knew it was all him. And he was all hers. His scent, his unique flavor, called to her like no other.

Absolute certainty that he was her mate filled her, and Anna understood his rush to claim her the night before. It humbled her and thrilled her at the same time. She shivered in response to the emotions washing over her in great tsunamic waves. Lance swapped skin for fur, his Shift much swifter and easier than hers.

It will get better, love, he whispered into her mind.

Her mate was large and strong, as handsome on four legs as he was on two.

Want. Need. Mine.

Yours, he snarled, *let's explore together. Then I will claim you again.*

Her stomach quivered at the suggestion. His voice was clear inside her head, where hers was mostly single words, but she knew that would change too over time. Sounded like a plan. Anna wanted him as badly as he did her.

Yes. Definitely. Always.

Grrr.

Before the moment grew too intense, Lance swatted her butt with the tip of his thick tail and took off. Her she-Cat yowled indignantly, giving chase. The snow was thick, covering the woods in a blanket of white, but her she-Tiger went wild for it.

She ran after snowflakes and caught them on her long, sand-papery tongue. All her senses had increased. The world was new and exciting like this, but she was still getting the hang of things on four legs.

She stopped at a stream to drink, and her

overzealous mate tackled her from behind. Annalia managed to stay on the shore, rolling on the bank. She stopped in prone position.

Waiting.

Lance grunted and leapt to her side. She felt his fear, worry, and anxiety as if they were her own. The joke she'd planned forgotten, she sprung up rushing to reassure him. The big Tiger heaved a breath and licked her face with the flat side of his rough tongue.

It was unlike anything she'd ever felt, but it was honest and good. For the first time in her life, Annalia understood what it was to be loved.

She knew now that Shifters were real, but she didn't know mating one would feel this way. Thank goodness for Uncle Uzzi. Running into the matchmaker had been the best damn thing that had ever happened to Anna.

But even in her wildest dreams, Anna had never expected this. Falling in love with her soulmate and turning into a Tiger—how did one prepare for such things? How did one adjust?

Together, Lance answered her unspoken questions.

Together, she echoed

Anna calmed immediately. He was a gift, she realized. As was turning into a Shifter. The best gifts she'd ever received in her whole life. His wintergreen scent wrapped around her like a warm, familiar blanket and she shivered and rubbed along his side.

It was time for them to go home.

Mine.

Chapter Seventeen

Before they'd showered—separately, to his great disappointment—Lance ordered enough Chinese food to feed an army. The delivery person had left it on the porch while they'd been dressing, but now, he was spreading the feast out on the dining table.

He hoped like hell he'd managed to get something she liked. Nerves assailed him. He was not used to having to work hard for female attention, but Annalia was so much more than anything he was used to.

He fidgeted with the wrapper on one of the seven egg rolls he'd ordered. Fuck it, he growled and ripped the paper. He did the same to all seven, putting them on a plate.

Shit.

Did that look messy? He was a fucking wreck here, and this was only dinner. How was he going to get through the rest of the evening if feeding her made him shake like a fucking cub?

"Hi," she said, coming into the room. Her voice soothed the tension that'd built inside of him.

Lance faced his mate and his heart stuttered. She was all pink and warm from her shower. Their run through the woods had been incredible. She took to her she-Tiger as if she'd been born one, and in a way she had. Created by the universe itself to be his fated mate, she was beyond his wildest imaginings.

Wrapped up in his bathrobe, Anna padded forward, and Lance almost swallowed his tongue. Her cherry chocolate scent was intoxicating, as was her expression. So open, so kind. Her damp curls corkscrewed around her face, and fuck, he was glad he'd thrown on a pair of sweatpants. Not that they hid his erection, but at least he didn't have to worry about it while he fed her.

"You ordered food?"

"Yeah, I thought you might be hungry."

"I am starving," she returned, and pride shot through him. He was happy to take care of her needs.

"The shift takes a lot out of you," he began, worried about this conversation.

"I am so sorry I didn't have a chance to explain—"

"I know," she said. "And you will get the chance, but let's eat first."

Annalia sat down across from him and handed him a plate. Those words meant everything to him, and he was grateful.

So fucking grateful, he damn near cried.

She was giving him a chance here. Now, all he had to do was not fuck it up. Lance accepted the plate from her, following her lead as she opened cartons and added some food to her dish. Everything she picked up, she offered him first. The gesture touched him, her consideration really. Generosity seemed to come naturally to her.

"This is good. Is it from a local place?"

"Uh, yeah," he nodded, trying hard to swallow the lump of nerves in his throat.

"Drink? I have beer, wine, soda, mineral water?"

"Can I have mineral water?"

"Sure." Lance got up and grabbed the glass bottle of imported mineral water along with two glasses.

After a while, Lance forgot his nervousness and just enjoyed the meal with her. Anna was easy to be with, and that caused him to wonder. Maybe his parents had it wrong, and mates could live in harmony together.

"So, about Tigers? Your family? I hardly know anything about you," she said.

"Well, my father left when I was still a cub, but Mom is still in my life," he explained. "She moved to South Carolina some years ago, but I talk to her every week."

"That must have been hard on you. Them splitting up," she said, and he felt her sympathy warm him.

"They were not true mates, and it was better that way. To stop my young Tiger from becoming too antisocial, my mother enlisted Hunter, he's our Pride Neta, to help."

Those were troubled times, but he'd dealt with his struggles and earned his place in the Pride house with blood, sweat, and tears. He was loyal to Hunter Maverick and the Pride. Couldn't fathom a time when they didn't come first, except now she was first.

"You mentioned you're a guard? What does that mean?"

"Well, the way Tiger Prides work is we have a leader, an alpha that we call the *Neta*. His mate is the *Nari,* and together they lead the group—"

"Wait, Tiger Shifter groups are called Prides? Like Lions?"

Lance hissed. He was not a fucking pansy-ass Lion. His inner beast rose, chuffed, and growled at the suggestion. But he backed off once he understood his mate was asking questions.

"No, not like *Lions*," he scoffed. "We are way cooler than Lions! Those overgrown house cats can't even comprehend our awesomeness."

"Is that so?" she laughed.

"Damn straight," he insisted, loving the sound of her laughter as she tried to stifle her giggles.

"Okay, easy. Tigers are cooler than Lions."

"Way cooler."

"Fine, way cooler. You happy now?"

"Yes," he said honestly, holding her gaze with his.

Was it him, or did the temperature just rise by about a hundred degrees? The robe she was wearing opened slightly as she wiggled in her seat. Giving him an unobstructed view of the swell of her breasts. Fuck beef and broccoli. Lance was hungry for something else.

His mate. And her amazing wonderland of a body.

She was soft and supple. All welcoming warmth and silky skin. Anna fit him like a glove. She smiled and bit her lip. brushing her still damp hair behind her ears. The movement caused the robe to open wider, baring more of her bountiful breasts to his starving eyes.

"Annalia," he growled her name and stood.

"Yeah," she raised her eyebrow tauntingly.

The little she-Cat knew exactly what she was doing. He stalked over to her side, turning her chair around. Lance tugged her upright by the knot in her belt and Annalia hissed through her teeth. The sound of her wild she-Cat made his cock even harder.

"Want you, mate," he rubbed his nose against hers.

"Really?" she grinned.

Lance nodded, nuzzling her face to the side, but the minx avoided his kiss. He followed the trail she laid out, but always, she evaded him at the end. The chase was sweet, but he'd had enough playing.

Lance grabbed the sides of the robe and pushed it off her shoulders, leaving it bunched at the belt around her waist. Annalia seemed to like his impatience. The scent of her excitement invaded his nostrils, and he growled harder.

Frustrated, and horny as fuck, he didn't let go of her belt, couldn't for fear he'd drop her as she leaned back. She trusted him to keep her upright as she cupped her own breasts, lifting them high for his pleasure.

"This what you want?" she teased.

He growled his response and Anna straightened once more. Lance reached for her, almost had her too. So close, his hands opened, but she skittered away.

"Lance?" she called out, squeezing, and fondling her nipples, moaning as she tugged on the hard nubbins. "Remember my rules, no touching till I say. Mmm, this feels so good."

Lance stood stock still. Holy shit. Anna was in the living room now. She opened the borrowed robe and let it fall, revealing every inch of her olive-toned skin to his hungry eyes.

Need pulsed through him, and it grew as her own lust-glazed eyes raked over his naked chest. She continued to moan and touch herself, pressing her mounds together. The sound of his Tiger's growl filled the room, but his minx was not finished taunting him. She walked backwards. Legs hitting the couch, Anna sat down.

"Come closer," she commanded, and his legs obeyed. "Far enough."

Grrr.

His Tiger was hanging on by a thread, but he was grateful for the few feet of space she granted him. Lance wanted to see just what his little Cat had planned.

Fucking hell, she was unbelievable. Anna moaned, rubbing her hands over her body. She fondled and played until she reached her knees. Then his little innocent Annalia parted her legs, pushing them wide, but painstakingly slow. Lance wouldn't, couldn't blink if he tried.

Her heavy breasts swayed as she remained slightly bent forward, blocking his view of her pussy. His chest rumbled with the force of his need. Louder still when she licked her supple lips.

"Annalia," he purred her name.

She was driving him wild. And she knew it too. It was there in the amber glint of her deep brown eyes. She beckoned him tugging on her breasts, like ripe cherries waiting to be plucked. Next, his sexy Anna moved her hands up her inner thighs.

Yesssss.

There it was. His prize. She drew a path in lazy circles with her fingertips. Lance followed the trail with his eyes greedily. He planned to do the same with his mouth, but contented himself watching her fingers continue their maddening route towards heaven. She sucked in a breath, tracing her glistening outer lips.

Lance's growl burst forth. More snarl now. But what was he supposed to do? She was wetting her fingertips with her own cream, moaning with delight while she petted her pretty pussy for his viewing pleasure.

"Mine," he snarled, and his vixen moved even faster.

Quick little circles around her clit followed by a rapid *tap, tap, tap*. Her mouth opened wide as she panted in time with her touches. His Tiger scratched and snarled.

That was his pussy, his clit, his cream.

Mine. Mine. MINE!

"Show me I'm yours, pussy cat."

Lance didn't have to be told twice.

He pounced.

Chapter Eighteen

Annalia was never what you would call a sex siren. She liked sex. Loved it, in fact. She just wasn't used to having good sex. At least, not with another person. But masturbation could only get a girl so far.

With Lance, all that changed. Her sexy, gorgeous Tiger watched her fondle and stroke her sex with greedy, hungry eyes. The second she gave him permission, he leapt across ten feet as if it were nothing, just to sink on all fours in front of her wide-open legs.

Lance knelt in front of her like a knight of old. Fuck, it was hot. He made her feel like some sort of deity to be worshipped. Annalia wasn't done taunting him yet. She slid her cream-soaked hands to his mouth, and he licked them one at a time. His intense growl made her even more wet.

She was taunting him, daring him to act. Never had she been so bold, never with anyone else. She couldn't even imagine it.

Anna had never stripped for her lover, touched herself for him. It wasn't in her nature to be so adventurous and daring. Well, it wasn't *before*. *Raw* and *dirty* were things she'd always been curious about.

But they were secret fantasies of hers. Sort of like having a gorgeous man kneel between her thick thighs. And Lance was fucking gorgeous. Big, sexy, and sweet and he wanted her. She knew it, reveled in it. Nothing felt as good as knowing he wanted her. Well, except for when he was touching her.

He inhaled deeply, holding in his breath as if to savor her scent. The way he wanted her was so fucking hot. With a subtle flex of her hips, she enticed him forward.

Need, arousal, burning lust, and buds of affection swelled up inside of her. Her sex clenched on air, begging to be filled. She'd started out teasing him, but now she was the one silently begging for his attentions.

She didn't know what came over her. Well, that

wasn't entirely true. She knew what, but some things were plain unbelievable. She pinched herself on her outer thigh, just to be certain.

"Mine," growled her mate.

Her pussy ached with the need to be filled. This level of desire was burning her alive. The she-Cat inside her hissed and growled. She wanted to get right down to the part where he fucked her stupid, filled her with his cubs, and they lived happily ever after.

Next, he leaned forward, his hot breath on her thigh, and all thought fled her brain. His tongue swept over her lips, parting them, sliding inside. He growled against her, making her vibrate with the force of the sound.

Fucking hell, the man was purring as he lapped at her center. Better than any vibrator. Head back, she moaned and rocked her hips in time with his licks.

Lance was a motherfucking cunnilingus god. He made her weak kneed with his carnal skills, but he really touched her heart with everything else he did. All the soulful stares and thoughtful questions he asked about her.

He supported her when she'd stood up to Sandra and Glenn. Not taking over, or trying to rescue her, he let her handle it. He believed she could, and that was amazing.

"Oh god," she moaned aloud as he added one finger, then two to her sheath.

Stroking them along her g-spot, Lance purred as he flicked her clit with his tongue. He used everything he had. Lips, tongue, fangs, fingers. Lance was not holding back, but he was taking his time.

Fuck, it was so good.

Purring loudly, the vibrations coming from his mouth rocked her like her own personal massager. And she loved every bit of it. Then he scraped one long fang along her swollen clit, and Annalia saw stars. She was one big explosion of pleasure.

Every single atom that made up her being scattered into oblivion. Pulling his hair, she held him in place, rocking her hips, pressing her pussy firmly to his mouth, riding out wave after wave of unending bliss.

He lifted his head, slowed the plundering of his fingers, and grinned. Evidence of her pleasure coated his lips and chin, but Annalia wasn't embarrassed. Still holding onto his hair, she pulled him forward.

Crushing her mouth to his, tasting her own desire on his lips, her hands traveled down his hard chest and the rippling muscles of his abs until she found it. His cock was long and thick, pulsing in his grip as she guided him to her slick, swollen heat.

Lance wasn't smiling anymore. Claws gripping her hips, he thrusted his pelvis forward until he filled her all the way to the hilt. The curve of her body hanging half-way off the couch allowed him to slide deep, so deep. Annalia's beast roared in pure joy.

"Yes," she moaned aloud, and clung to his shoulders with her sharp nails digging into his skin.

"Mine," his voice was no more than gasps, but she loved it, needed it.

The stark possession in the word called to her she-Cat. She wanted to be his, knew it was where she belonged. The absolute certainty stunned her, but she welcomed it. How marvelous to be so sure, and hell yes, she was sure.

Lance was her fated mate, and she was his.

Mine, mine, mine.

He growled and moaned with each thrust, pulling whimpers and cries from her lips as his massive cock stroked every nerve ending inside her slick sheath. Cupping her ass, he lifted her higher until he was standing.

"Shit, I'm too heavy," she worried aloud, wrapping her legs around his waist.

"You're fucking perfect," he growled and pressed her up against the wall.

Arms wrapped around his neck, she kissed his mouth as he continued to move. The ridges along his cock stroked her sensitive flesh as he drove in and out of her heat.

Fuck, fuck, fuck.

Her pleasure grew and her she-Tiger surged forward. It had to be at the right moment. She knew that instinctively. The moment her orgasm began, her sheath tightened around his cock, gripping him like a vise. Then Annalia struck.

Wrapping her jaws around his right shoulder, she pierced his tender flesh, giving him her mating mark. Lance cried out. His cock grew bigger, harder inside of her with the strength of his orgasm.

The beast roared proudly as blood filled her mouth, hot and sweet with hints of his own wintergreen scent. She swallowed it down like the animal she was, then released him, and licked the wounds closed.

Still trembling with the force of their coming together, Lance somehow managed to get them to the bedroom.

"That was," she was still panting, trying to get a hold of her breathing.

"Yeah," he nuzzled her cheek, "Need your pump?"

"No," she smiled, and meant it.

This breathlessness was entirely welcome.

Epilogue

"What if they don't like me?"

"How could anyone not like you?" Lance looked at his gorgeous mate as if she'd lost her freaking mind.

"I don't know, Lance, I am not exactly a people person."

"Baby, you are amazing, and you're mine. They will love you."

He still couldn't believe she'd said yes. Sure, he'd jumped the gun when he'd claimed her. Hadn't at all explained what it meant to be his. After she'd gone through the *Puspa*, he thought for sure, she'd be pissed as hell.

But Annalia surprised him at every turn. Beautiful and curvy goddess that she was. He'd spent the morning raining kisses along her soft skin. The spicy chocolate cherry taste of her forever imbedded on his tongue.

He thanked the gods, *and Uncle Uzzi*, for bringing them together. Of course, there was still a lot they needed to learn about each other, but she was willing to try, and that meant everything to him. Lance was not going to fuck this up.

"I called the company Sandra used to pack my things. Instead of returning them to the apartment, they will be at the cabin sometime tomorrow, if that's okay?"

"Okay? That's perfect, love," he replied and flashed that wicked grin she seemed to love so much.

"Good," she said, but she was nervous.

"What's wrong?" Lance frowned.

"I guess, I am just worried about my sister, about us. A lot of changes, you know?"

"Yeah," he commiserated and placed a hand on her thigh, squeezing gently. "But you don't have to go through any of it alone. I am here for you."

"I know." She smiled at him, and there it was, Lance's own personal ray of sunshine.

Her curly brown hair was down today, and he loved the way the spiral tendrils framed her face.

Absolutely beautiful.

"What?"

"Just thinking how lucky I am."

"Yeah right," she snorted and even that was charming, "Wow, look at all this snow!"

He'd called Brayden that morning about keeping the company mode of transportation, and the Beta had agreed it wasn't a problem. It wasn't his range Rover, but it would do the job.

"Sorry about your car," she bit her lip, picking up on his thoughts.

"Don't even worry about it, love. I ordered a new one already."

"It was all your fault anyway," she said and tried for haughty, but his mate was all giggles once his fingers found her ribs.

He lifted her up and pulled her over onto his lap, tickling her then kissing her some more. Someone knocked on the window, and they broke apart.

"You two coming inside or what?"

"Who is that?" Annalia whispered, tiny hands clutched at his shoulders.

"That's just Pierce," he said, and nodded at the man, "In a minute, bro."

Lance wasn't rushing her. He just held her and waited until she was breathing normally again. The she-Cat would take care of most of her allergies, but she'd been born a human. Her asthma was still going to be an issue, though nowhere near as bad as before.

"I'm fine," she told him.

"You sure?"

"Yes." She pushed against him. "Come on."

Lance walked into the Pride House first. Hand on the small of his mate's back, he guided her to the large living room. He liked the feel of the soft ivory sweater she wore over dark brown leggings and knee-high boots.

The fire was roaring and the curtains that covered the sliding doors leading outside were open, revealing the gorgeous snow-covered yard. A couple of Tigers prowled outside, playing in the white fluff, and Annalia gasped. He had to remember she wasn't used to such sights, even if she was one of them now.

"Hi!" the Nari walked in with two babies on her hip, and promptly handed one over to his mate, "I'm Elissa, and you are Anna, right? Would you mind? Celia has been cranky all day."

"Not at all," Annalia smiled at the little cherub, her nerves disappearing at once.

Lance nodded his thanks and Elissa winked as she handed little Melly to him. The Nari was a kickass female and knew exactly how to break the ice.

"Thank you both. I made some snacks earlier," she said and smiled. "I'll just get them."

"Sure, thank you," his sweet mate answered.

They sat down on the rug with the precious cubs and Lance pulled a chest filled with toys over so they could play. Little by little, more of the Pride came in to meet her. They were just amazing with her. No one was pushy or rushing her in any way. He just sat back and watched his Annalia blossom.

Lance cleared his throat and nodded his thanks to Hunter and Elissa. They'd brought in a couple of trays filled with homemade goodies.

"Wow, these are great," Annalia said and took a second bite of the small beef and potato stuffed empanada.

"Thanks, I was a personal chef before I became the Nari," Elissa told her and grinned. "Now, I guess I am the personal chef for the whole Pride."

"Thank the gods for that," Reg said and laughed with his arm around his very pregnant mate, Gretchen.

"Amen," Brayden said, holding his own little cub. "We used to take turns, and it wasn't good."

"Hell, I made a mean chili," Lance insisted.

"Yeah," Hunter said and laughed. "If by mean you mean terrible."

They all giggled then and spent the next hour chatting pleasantly. Someone brought in a board game, and soon they had a wicked round of Uno going. Pierce grumbled after losing twice in a row, but everyone just laughed as the last single member of the Honor Guard stormed away.

Couples came and went until it was just the two of them and the Neta and Nari once more.

"Annalia, we understand you have experienced the *Puspa,* and are now a Shifter," Hunter began. "As Lance's mate, you would have been an honorary member anyway, but since you are now a Shifter, we would like to officially welcome you to our Pride."

"That means you are family, sweetheart," Elissa said and teared up. The Nari pulled the younger woman in for a big hug.

"Thank you," Annalia swallowed and hugged her back. "I haven't really had that before, but I promise I will make you both glad I am here."

"we already are," Elissa reassured her, and Lance's heart warmed watching the two females bond.

Anna wasn't used to that sort of thing. He knew from the way she talked about life with her sister. Sandra and Glenn were not exactly dripping affection. But his Annalia deserved that and more.

She will get used to it, he promised himself.

Because like it or not, she was his now, and he was going to spoil her rotten with how much he loved her. Love filled him as the Nari whispered words of comfort, promises of friendship, and most of all, happiness as she told his Anna that she belonged right there with them. For Always.

"The Pride is a family like nothing you have ever known. We have our squabbles, but we will always have your back."

"Thank you, I, I don't know what to say," Anna replied and wiped her eyes.

Lance knew what she was feeling. Through their matebond, he was keenly aware of her emotions. Truth was, he was quite overwhelmed himself.

The Pride had not only welcomed his mate with open arms, but they cared for her already. It was there in the link that connected all the Tigers of Maverick Point. He'd never been so honored in his life.

Except, of course, when she'd said yes.

Mine.

That night, Annalia welcomed Lance's arms around her. The day had gone better than she'd expected. The Pride was wonderful, and she just knew Elissa, Jessica, Pamela, Gretchen, and Kylie were going to be amazing friends.

Already, she had a lesson in *how-to-be-a-kickass-she-Cat* scheduled with her new Nari. Smirking, she snuggled deeper into Lance, who she'd thought was still asleep. The bulging evidence at her back said otherwise, of course. Thank god.

"Mate," he purred into her ear, the sound eliciting an instant response.

Pussy dampening, Annalia moaned and pressed against him again. The she-Cat couldn't get enough of her big, protective, sexy male.

Good mate. Strong. Ours.

The human side of her was quick to agree. She understood the link that bound them was more perfect than any human license or declaration, and yet...

"Lance," she moaned his name as he slid his cock between her thighs, along the crack of her ass, grazing her outer lips in a slick, sensuous tease.

"Yeah?" he growled.

The flex of his hips increased, and moisture

pooled between her legs. She pushed back, trying to get him where she wanted.

Fucking sweet torture, she moaned.

Anna wanted him inside her, filling her, fucking her, making her come. He was her fated mate. That instinct that drove him to the source of her pleasure was un-fucking-canny. He would always know how to touch her, where to kiss her, and when to strike.

With one enormous hand, he captured her breast, rolling the nipple between his fingers, and Anna moaned. His fangs scraped over the mating mark he'd given her and sent shockwaves of heat straight to her pussy.

"Need," he whispered.

Licking and sucking her skin, his dick continued to tease her slit. Anna knew then things would never be any more perfect than when he was with her.

All her childhood fantasies came flooding into her brain, so, she decided, why the hell not?

"Will you marry me?"

The second the words spilled from her lips her mate stopped moving. Her heart thudded inside her chest. Did she read him wrong? Fuck. Why did she open her mouth?

"Uh, you don't have to," she said and tried back-tracking, "It's stupid. I'm sorry I mentioned it."

But Lance had her turned over, and himself situated between her thighs before she could finish the thought. His blue orbs glowed with his beast and his entire body trembled like a leaf on a tree. The snowstorm raging outside was nothing compared to the battle she saw taking place within him.

"Do you mean it?" his voice was thick with his beast and the emotions riding him.

"What?"

"Did you mean it when you asked me to marry you?"

Annalia swallowed the lump in her throat. Fuck it. She wasn't a coward. It might seem ridiculous to the people who knew her. Hell, she had a tough time believing it herself, but the fact was this man was her fated mate, and what's more, she was completely in love with him.

Nodding her head, she opened her mouth to tell him everything.

"Yes, I meant it, but—"

But that was as far as she got before he was filling her pussy, stretching it with his cock, and crashing his lips to hers. Lance made love to her like a wild man.

"Yes."

Every time he touched her, it was more intense

than the last. The sensations growing felt better and better. Her own she-Cat rose, taking this love-making as the affirmation it was.

"Yes," he said again.

She needed him. Like as in needed, needed. The seeds of affection had taken root, were growing each minute they spent together. And maybe it was silly, but she wanted to marry him.

She always thought adults had no use for fairy-tales. Her parents' death left her sister in charge of raising her, and Sandra was not a very imaginative or demonstrative person. But Anna had always dreamt of her true love.

Now that she'd found him, she wanted to stand up in front of a crowd and speak her vows. She wanted a real wedding with a dress, and a cake, and doves. The whole shebang.

"Yes. Yes. A hundred times yes," Lance purred while he drove into her. "You are mine, Annalia. Mine. Mate. Soon to be wife."

"You'll marry me?" she asked again, the pleasure building inside of her was growing so intense at his words.

"Fuck, yes," he promised.

She pushed against his chest, using her hips and newfound strength to flip positions. Once astride, she sat up. His hands reached up to cup her breasts, and she took a moment to adjust to the even deeper invasion of his incredible length.

He grunted as she lifted and slammed back down, impaling herself. Together they moved, a communion of bodies and souls, and she'd never felt so perfectly in tune with another being. But Lance was hers, and she was his. And this was only the beginning.

Her love swelled within her, she acknowledged the feeling, knew in her heart it was true as his love was for her.

"Love you, mate," he sat up, pressing his hungry mouth to hers.

It was more than a kiss. It was like oxygen. She needed it to live. Breathing him in, tasting him with her tongue, filling her womb with his seed as they rocked each other into another world, Annalia gorged herself on him.

"You're all I will ever need," he said, "Love you. Wanna marry you. I'll be your husband, and you will be my wife. My mate, my love, my best friend," he whispered as they held each other.

"I love you," she said, and the truth of her words filled her with peace.

Inside her mind's eye, she saw her she-Tiger with

his own magnificent animal. Together they lay under the shade of a tree in that metaphysical plane where the two existed. Their matebond pulsed around them, a thick blue rope that glowed with love and happiness.

Life was full of changes and turns, the unexpected was about the only thing a person could count on. Annalia had not been lucky for most of her life, but this, this blew everything else away.

"This is just the beginning," Lance whispered.

"It's been *purrfect* so far," she grinned.

And she meant it. They were *purrfectly bound* as one unit, one love, mates forever.

The end.

Uncle Uzzi stretched as he looked through his mail. One thick envelope stood out among the rest.

"How nice," he smiled as he read the invitation.

Spring Weddings were lovely. He had just the gift for Annalia and Lance too. Since neither one of them was a good chef, they'd no doubt appreciate the cookbook filled with his liebling's own recipes and the brand new 6-quart Insta-pot he planned to send.

The Maverick Pride was growing in leaps and bounds. One of Uzzi's most successful groups, he mused. His blue gaze travelled over the other pile of letters, and a frown touched his face as he came across one of his itineraries.

Whenever travelling the Garden State, Uncle Uzzi chose to be driven by Falcon Limousine Service with Hank, the business' owner, as his trusted driver. But it looked like Hank was taking a hiatus.

Hmm.

Hank Garrett was the son of a very good friend of Uncle Uzzi's from long ago. He'd worked hard to build his company and only drove him around himself because of that relationship. And yet, he'd refused his offer, stating repeatedly, he needed no help finding his mate.

But the clock was ticking for the Falcon Shifter. Eventually, he'd be calling, and as always, Uncle Uzzi would be ready.

"I know what you need, Hank Garret," he clucked his tongue to his empty apartment.

"Stop being so stubborn. Fate is unavoidable."

Did you enjoy this story? Check out the rest of the Maverick Pride Tales today! And keep on the lookout for more titles in this steamy PNR series.

& You can expect the new edition of Shake That Sass and a brand new take on The Wyvern Protection Unit real soon!
And do not forget to look for Hank's story in Purrfectly Paired coming soon.

PURRFECTLY PAIRED

C.D. GORRI

Polar Outbreak
Polar Compound
Polar Curve

and, of course, the Barvale Holiday Tales, beginning
with A Bear For Christmas
Hers to Bear
Thank You Beary Much
&
Bearing Gifts!
Look for more of these sexy, heartwarming holiday
inspired tales soon!

No cliffhangers. Steamy PNR fun.
Go and read your next happily ever after today!

Beware... here be Dragons!

The Falk Clan Tales are my stories surrounding four Dragon Shifter brothers and how they find their one true mates!

Each brother's chest is marked with his rose, the magical link to his heart and his magic. They each have a matching gemstone to go with it.

In *The Dragon's Valentine* we meet the eldest Falk brother, Callius. He is on a mission to find a Castle and his one true mate, one he can trust with his diamond rose....

She's given up on love, but he's just begun...

In *The Dragon's Christmas Gift* our attention shifts to Alexsander, the youngest brother of the four. He has resigned himself to a life alone, until he meets *her…*

His heart is frozen. Can she change his mind about love?

The Dragon's Heart is the story of Edric Falk who has vowed never to love again, but that changes when he meets his feisty mate, Joselyn Curacao.

Some wounds run deep. Can a Dragon's heart be unbroken?

Meet Nikolai Falk in the last Falk Clan Tale, *The Dragon's Secret.*

She just wants a little fun, he's looking for a lifetime.

*These first four books are now available in one convenient set. Look for Dragon Mates today.

Meet another long lost Falk brother in *The Dragon's Treasure.* Castor Falk breaks free from his prison in search of his kin, he finds his mate instead.

She doesn't believe in fairytales, until a Dragon comes knocking on her door.

The Dragon's Surprise features a new Dragon, Devine Graystone, and a female Werewolf who makes him think twice about his lonely state of being...

Nothing can surprise this six hundred-year-old Dragon, except maybe her.

Lastly, in *The Dragon's Dream* we meet a spunky she-Wolf who gives Nicholas Graystone a run for his money when it comes to romance. Can a Dragon really have it all?

He's a hardcore realist until she dares him to dream.

Wolf Bride: The Story of Ailis and Eoghan A Macconwood Pack Tale 1

Summer Bite: A Macconwood Pack Tale 2

His Winter Mate: A Macconwood Pack Tale 3

Snow Angel: A Macconwood Pack Tale 4

Charley's Baby Surprise: A Macconwood Pack Tale 5

Home for the Howlidays: A Macconwood Pack Tale 6

A Silver Wedding: A Macconwood Pack Tale 7

Mine Furever: A Macconwood Pack Tale 8

A Furry Little Christmas: A Macconwood Pack Tale 9

Also available in two boxed sets:

The Macconwood Pack Tales Volume 1

Shifters Furever: The Macconwood Pack Tales Volume 2

The Falk Clan Tales:

The Dragon's Valentine: A Falk Clan Novel 1

The Dragon's Christmas Gift: A Falk Clan Novel 2

The Dragon's Heart: A Falk Clan Novel 3

The Dragon's Secret: A Falk Clan Novel 4

The Dragon's Treasure: A Falk Clan Novel 5

The Dragon's Surprise: A Falk Clan Novel 6

The Dragon's Dream: A Falk Clan Novel 7

Dragon Mates: The Falk Clan Series Boxed Set Books 1-4

<u>The Bear Claw Tales:</u>

Bearly Breathing: A Bear Claw Tale 1

Bearly There: A Bear Claw Tale 2

Bearly Tamed: A Bear Claw Tale 3

Bearly Mated: A Bear Claw Tale 4

Also available in a boxed set:

The Complete Bear Claw Tales (Books 1-4)

<u>The Barvale Clan Tales:</u>

Polar Opposites: The Barvale Clan Tales 1

Polar Outbreak: The Barvale Clan Tales 2

Polar Compound: A Barvale Clan Tale 3

Polar Curve: A Barvale Clan Tale 4

Also available in a boxed set:

The Barvale Clan Tales (Books 1-4)

<u>Barvale Holiday Tales:</u>

A Bear For Christmas

Hers To Bear

Thank You Beary Much

Bearing Gifts

Also available in a boxed set:

The Barvale Holiday Tales (Books 1-3)

<u>Purely Paranormal Romance Books:</u>

Marked by the Devil: Purely Paranormal Romance Books

Mated to the Dragon King: Purely Paranormal Romance Books

Claimed by the Demon: Purely Paranormal Romance Books

Christmas with a Devil, a Dragon King, & a Demon: Purely Paranormal Romance Books

Vampire Lover: Purely Paranormal Romance Books

Grizzly Lover: Purely Paranormal Romance Books

Christmas With Her Chupacabra: Purely Paranormal Romance Books

Purely Paranormal Romance Books Anthology

The Wardens of Terra:

Bound by Air: The Wardens of Terra Book 1

Star Kissed: A Wardens of Terra Short

Waterlocked: The Wardens of Terra Book 2

Moon Kissed: A Wardens of Terra Short

*Now in a boxed set and in audio!

The Maverick Pride Tales:

Purrfectly Mated

Purrfectly Kissed

Purrfectly Trapped

Purrfectly Caught

Purrfectly Naughty

Purrfectly Bound

Dire Wolf Mates:

Shake That Sass

Breaking Sass

Pinch of Sass

Kickin' Sass

Wyvern Protection Unit:

Gift Wrapped Protector: WPU 1

Standalones:

The Enforcer

Blood Song: A Sanguinem Council Book

Spring Fling (co-written with P. Mattern)

EveL Worlds:

Chinchilla and the Devil: A FUCN'A Book

Sammi and the Jersey Bull: A FUCN'A Book

Mouse and the Ball: A FUCN'A Book

The Guardians of Chaos:

Wolf Shield: Guardians of Chaos Book 1

Dragon Shield: Guardians of Chaos Book 2

Stallion Shield: Guardians of Chaos Book 3

Panther Shield: Guardians of Chaos 4

Witch Shield: Guardians of Chaos 5

Mated to the Werewolf Next Door: A Howl's Romance

The Tiger King's Christmas Bride

Claiming His Virgin Mate: Howls Romance

Doubly Claimed

Doubly Bound

Doubly Tied

Shifter Mountain: Hearts of Stone 1

Shifter City: Hearts of Stone 2

Shifter Village: Hearts of Stone 3

Fangs For Nothin'

Moongate Island Mate

Moongate Island Christmas Claim

Mated by Moonlight

Ash: Speed Dating with the Denizens of Underworld

Arachne: Speed Dating with the Denizens of Underworld

<u>Hungry Fur Love</u>

Hungry Like Her Wolf: Magic and Mayhem Universe

Hungry For Her Bear: Magic and Mayhem Universe

<u>Shifters Unleashed Boxed Sets</u>

Check out these amazing anthologies where you can find some of my books and the works of other awesome authors!

Midnight Magic Anthology (Water Witch)

Rituals & Runes Anthology (Air Witch)

<u>Island Stripe Pride</u>

Tiger Claimed

Tiger Denied

<u>NYC Shifter Tales</u>

Cuff Linked

Sealed Fate

<u>A Howlin' Good Fairytale Retelling</u>

Sweet As Candy (as seen in Once Upon An Ever After)

<u>Coming Soon:</u>

Asterion

Vampire Shield: Guardians of Chaos 6

Tiger Rejected

For Fangs Sake

Hungry As Her Python: Magic and Mayhem Universe

If The Shoe Fits: A Howlin' Good Fairytale Retelling

Chickee and the Paparazzi: FUCN'A

The Wolf's Winter Wish: A Macconwood Pack Tale

The Hybrid Assassin

Tempted By Her Protector: WPU 2

Alien Protector: WPU 3

Elvish Protector: WPU 4

Thrilled By Her Protector: WPU 5

Young Adult Urban Fantasy Books:

Wolf Moon: A Grazi Kelly Novel Book 1

Hunter Moon: A Grazi Kelly Novel Book 2

Rebel Moon: A Grazi Kelly Novel Book 3

Winter Moon: A Grazi Kelly Novel Book 4

Chasing The Moon: A Grazi Kelly Short 5

Blood Moon: A Grazi Kelly Novel 6

*Get all 6 books NOW AVAILABLE IN A BOXED SET:

The Complete Grazi Kelly Novel Series

Casting Magic: The Angela Tanner Files 1

Keeping Magic: The Angela Tanner Files 2

G'Witches Magical Mysteries Series

Co-written with P. Mattern

G'Witches

G'Witches 2: The Harpy Harbinger

G'Witches 3: Summoning Secrets

Excerpt from *Wolf Shield: Guardians of Chaos*

What a day! Fergie McAndrews headed towards the pick-up truck she'd borrowed from her roommate for work that morning.

Of course, the thirty-thousand dollar certified used luxury car she'd splurged on earlier in the year was in the shop. Again.

Just another in a long line of bad decisions. After leaving a perfectly good job for a startup company, she was laid off three weeks ago and had to borrow money from her parents to pay rent. Wasn't that humiliating?

"This is the last time, Ferg," her step-monster had said after she'd Venmo'd the money to her.

God forbid the mechanic call and tell her the car

was ready. She wouldn't be able to pick it up for another week. That was when she got her first paycheck from her newest gig at L-Corp. Not a startup, but an older company with new offices in Bayonne, which was only a half-hour commute.

But to commute, you needed a car. Fergie had no choice but to borrow the old pick-up from her best friend and roommate, Jessenia Banks. It wasn't like she needed the truck. She worked from home these days. Besides, Fergie promised to fill it up and have it washed.

She huffed out a breath. It'd been a really long day. A crappy one too. Fergie wanted to love her new job. Really, she did. But so far, it was the pits. If Fergie wanted to be a librarian, she would've been one.

Research was her jam. Well, when it was interesting. She had a knack for sniffing out information and compiling easy-to-read spreadsheets and time-lines. It wasn't the hard work that annoyed her. Her complaint was the content. The actual stuff her new boss had her looking up. It was beyond boring.

Why an enormous conglomerate like L-Corp needed old land surveys, cross-referenced with newspaper reports on accidents, crimes, etcetera.

She had no idea. She'd been at it for weeks now. So far, she'd researched six locations given via GPS coordinates across Hudson County. Her new boss wanted everything, every little insignificant piece of information she could dig up.

That was the easy part. It was the hassle of the actual job that really made her want to give up. Every day she had to drive to Bayonne to pick up her work laptop she'd dropped off the night before with all of that day's findings. Every single night they wiped her computer clean.

Like she was going to run away with the secrets of what happened on 2nd and Washington sixty-years ago. Can you say paranoid? Ugh.

Fergie had always looked forward to working for a huge global company. It was supposed to be her ticket out of the Garden State. Traveling the globe, seeing new things, visiting far-off places was always a secret dream of hers. Well, that, and having her own walk-in closet full of gorgeous designer shoes.

Best secret dream evah! In her opinion, anyway. What woman didn't love shoes? Fergie hummed as she daydreamed about rows and rows of Blahnik's, Jimmy Choo's, Garavani's, Ferragamo's, and her personal favorites, Louboutin's on every shelf!

Don't judge. Fergie wasn't shallow, she just liked pretty things. Haters gonna hate. But every time she ran across a thrift or second-chance store, she'd search high and low to see what they had. That was how she'd scored the pumps on her feet.

They made her feel good about herself. Being five-foot two-inches short with more curves than a racetrack, Fergie had had more than her fair share of self-esteem issues growing up. Alright, so she was chubby. She could admit that proudly now.

If everyone looked the same, the world would be one boring as hell place. Fergie liked herself perfectly fine these days, in spite of all the times her step-monster tried to make her diet growing up. So she liked food and shoes. Big deal.

She worked hard to feed and clothe herself, so as far as she was concerned, no one had a right to comment. So what if she wanted some excitement in her life? Fergie was aware she was better off than most, but what was wrong with having goals?

She'd spent a lot of time thinking about how a woman like her could have an adventure. Travelling was the only thing she could think of. Of course, she'd been hoping this job would be the answer to that. Even travelling for work was better than being stuck.

Sigh.

So far, her plans had fallen flat, but hey, at least she was earning a paycheck. Her new boss, Mr. Offner, might be a strange man, but he signed her checks, and that was enough for now. Fergie had never seen more than a glimpse of him. All of her instructions usually came via email.

Most of the time she was able to compile her research quickly, then she'd head back to the office to organize it into neat little spreadsheets, and finally, she'd hand it all in with her laptop. But not today.

Mr. Offner sent her an email detailing everything she could dig up on one of the oldest places on record in the county. Of course, land surveys that old, along with police reports, newspaper articles, deeds, and sales records were nowhere she could easily access them.

After wasting hours at both the court house and municipal building, Fergie had been directed to the *second* public library. Apparently anything over a hundred years old was filed away in the godforsaken place. She'd been shocked to find an entire room filled with musty old archives. And wouldn't you know it, there was no cell service and no internet access. Plus, their phone lines were down. She'd had to photograph each page using her cell. When she got home later, she would send those photos like a fax to her boss along with her spreadsheet. If she could manage that before collapsing into bed.

How the fuck did I wind up here?

It was all Elissa could do not to slam her face down on the table as she pondered that question for the umpteenth time since leaving her cozy Hoboken apartment to go on this so called date.

"So, babe," the over-stuffed, heavily-cologned, and downright fugly man said.

Her date of the evening looked like something out of a bad sitcom as he tried to lean over the stained tablecloth of the rundown hotel buffet room, he'd driven two hours to get to. Waggling his caterpillar-like eyebrows, he gave her the once over and Elissa's skin crawled.

Oh, hell no.

"I got a room upstairs, you know, for *after*," he

told her, nodding his head, and biting his lower lip in a manner she assumed he thought was provocative.

At best, it was nauseating.

FML.

How was this guy Elissa's date for the evening? What had she done to deserve this?

Little Gianni. Yup, that was how he'd introduced himself. And here she was. On a blind date with a guy who had the word 'little' in front of his name.

Well, what did she expect? Roses and champagne? In this economy? She didn't know where Cinder-fucking-ella got her prince, but it sure as fuck wasn't in Jersey.

Elissa could only blame herself for agreeing to go on this blind date. Initially, the whole Little Gianni fiasco had been intended for her roommate.

Wait a second. Scratch that thought.

It *was* all Gretchen's fault. That ungrateful cow!

She tried to play it off like she was some sweet little homegrown maiden. Oh, just wait till Elissa got home. Gretchen was never going to hear the end of it.

She owed Elissa. Big time. Like a whole month of washing the dishes big time. The rat trap they shared in her hometown of Hoboken was all the two women could afford, and for the most part, they got along just fine.

In fact, they'd grown to be close friends over the three years they'd lived together. It was the only reason she'd ever agreed to this date from Hell.

Elissa sighed and looked over at Little Gianni. Maybe he wasn't all that bad?

"*BEEEELLLLLLLLCHHH!* 'Scuse me, doll. Better out, am I right?"

Gianni winked and Elissa wished for a black hole to open up and swallow her up right through the floor.

OMFG.

The man just burped out loud like he was in a frat boy belting contest, only those days passed him up about thirty years ago.

For fuck's sake. Gretchen, you so owe me.

Elissa cursed her roommate and tried not to groan. But Little Gianni wasn't quite done. The grown ass man lifted his leg and let one rip.

Right. Fucking. There.

Elissa was going to die before the end of the night.

Literally.

This is what you get when you do a friend a favor without asking for details! Idiota!

The voice of her Italian grandmother sounded in her brain. She tried to ignore it, willing herself not to wince at the man while he sucked air, and who knows what else, noisily through his coffee-stained teeth.

Ew. So gross.

That was the perfect word to describe it. The only word, in fact. The entire date was just so fucking gross. She still couldn't believe her sweet little roommate from Iowa, *Gretchen Kaepernick*, she of the wispy hair and baby blues, had set her up with this guy!

What the actual fuck was up with that?

Little Gianni was a slob. Actually, he looked just like her Uncle Nico, and that was not a good thing. Seriously, not good at all.

He wore his hair slicked back in a too tight pony-tail that emphasized his rapidly receding hairline. As if that wasn't enough to put her off, he was sporting an enormous paunch. Now, being a curvy girl, Elissa appreciated food and was in no way against men showing the same appreciation.

She liked bigger men. Always had. But bigger did not mean you had to be sloppy. Little Gianni's stomach was literally hanging out from under a tight tan golf shirt that had definitely seen better days.

The man didn't even look like he had ever played a sport of any kind. With it, he wore brown polyester pants that were three inches above his ankles and unbuttoned at the waist.

He didn't look like he tried at all for this date. What kind of guy did that? His shirt collar was bent and wrinkled, and all three buttons were open to his chest, revealing a mat of oily, dark hair and pimples.

Somehow, he'd managed to tuck the back of the shirt in, but the front simply would not hold in that stomach. What worried her more were the tight brown pants.

As he sat back and stretched, she wondered if she should take cover. They looked like they were one bite from exploding off his body. Elissa shuddered at the image.

Please God, if You have an ounce of mercy, don't let that happen, she prayed.

"Hang on, doll, I gotta take this," he said, and turned to answer his cell phone.

It was ringing to the tune of '70s disco music she hadn't heard since the last family reunion. Her eyes kept going to the huge stain on the front of his shirt. It was a little game she liked to call *what the hell is that.*

Coffee, she guessed.

"Up your ass, Bruno. I gotta have it by Monday," he cursed into the receiver.

Elissa winced at the spectacle he was making of them both. There were only a handful of people there, but still.

Deep breaths.

Ew. Maybe not.

She coughed as the strong body spray, that he'd obviously used a ton of in lieu of a shower, bad move in her opinion, invaded her lungs.

Oh, this was so bad.

Elissa was, by no means, a snob. But this guy looked like he'd stepped out of a bad 1980s mafia spoof film. What's worse, he kept smacking his lips together as he hung up the phone and looked her over from head to chest.

Thank fuck for the table, she thought, wishing she could hide her bosoms from his view.

"Ssssss," he hissed, like it was sexy or something.

She just grimaced. Elissa might be able to forgive a lot of quirks, but she hated mouth noises. Really hated them. It was a super pet peeve of hers. Never mind his totally inappropriate and unwelcomed leer.

She started counting the minutes, willing the date to be over already. Plenty of people would tell her she shouldn't be so choosy, but really? She was not this desperate.

Not yet anyway.

So, she was curvy and a little mouthy too. But was it wrong to want a man with good table manners? Even if men were thin on the ground for someone like her.

As a chef, she'd worked in a lot of restaurants and even as a personal cook for professional couples. She'd seen her fair share of unhappy couples and downright uncomfortable marriages. But as far as she was concerned, all relationships went downhill when good table manners were dismissed.

Good manners were merely a sign that a person was thoughtful and respectful. At least, that was what Nonna had told her. Gianni here had clearly missed that lesson as a child. Elissa had to work not to groan in disgust as he slurped a raw clam down his gullet.

Shudder.

Was there no end to his feeding? That's what it reminded her of. Feeding time at the zoo.

OMG. That was rude, she scolded herself. But it wasn't like she said it out loud.

All she wanted to do was go home. At least she was comfortable. *She'd* worn her softest pair of black leggings for this disaster date, paired with one of her favorite tunics on top.

It was dark green with tiny black buttons down the front and showed just the right amount of cleavage. She'd gone for neat and tidy as opposed to downright sexy.

Good call, in her opinion. Elissa looked perfectly fine for a nice *getting to know you* dinner, which is what she thought she was getting when her roommate asked her to step in for her on a blind date that one of her best client's had set up for her.

Elissa shuddered now, thinking how good old Gianni here would've reacted to the red dress and heels she'd contemplated before checking the weather report.

Gulp.

The lewd man was already salivating, and she was so not having it. Fending off his unwanted advances was not how she wanted to finish the night.

Ew again.

Elissa shivered, slightly chilled despite the fact they were indoors. It was a cold, gloomy evening, and the forecast called for even more rain later that night. Not at all unusual for this time of year in the Garden State.

November was always chilly in the evenings, rainy too. Elissa tended to run warm, but she was glad she'd brought a jacket with her. Especially since her date refused to turn the heat on in the car.

When she'd asked, he'd looked offended and told her it wasted gas.

Um. Okay.

She checked her phone. It was only seven o'clock, but the two hour drive was still ahead of them. Maybe they could make it home before ten if they left soon.

Ugh. Did he just blow his nose?

"Allergies, doll. Say, you gonna eat that?" he asked before scooping a fry from her dish and swallowing it down.

Elissa was gonna kill her roomie. Gretchen was a hair and nail stylist. A lot of her clients were elderly, and they just loved her. They were always offering to set her up on blind dates with their nephews and grandsons.

Mostly, the sweet old ladies were kind. They swore they could find her curvy roommate the right man, assuming she was single because she was new to town. Well, when Elissa got home tonight, she was going to tell Gretchen she needed to fire the old lady who set this date up from being her client.

Like *ASAP*.

No one who liked Gretchen would've sent her out with this guy. Gianni reached over and touched her hand and Elissa pulled back, reaching for the napkin.

Gross.

"I sure hope you ain't a cold one, doll," he said, shaking his head.

"What?"

"Ain't gonna matter. I know just what you need, doll."

She was still wiping the greasy residue he'd transferred to her skin from the food he ate sans utensils. This was too much. Elissa was beyond uncomfortable with all the leering and bad attempts at innuendo.

Plus, she was starving. One look at the dump he'd taken her to, and she knew she could never eat there. The chef in her wouldn't allow it.

To think they drove two hours for this! She'd practically frozen to death in his maroon Cadillac, listening to a CD of the Rat Pack, while Gianni crooned loudly, and off key, to the music.

Normally, she was a fan of the famous group of legendary singers. Having grown up in Hoboken, she couldn't not be a Sinatra fan. Though, to be honest, Dean Martin had always been her favorite.

Still, Elissa was a firm believer that there were just some people you did not try to imitate. Especially not if you were Little Gianni. While he was belting his heart out, he'd been trying to get his right hand on her thigh. She'd asked him politely to stop.

Twice.

Then she'd been forced to try something a little more drastic. Like spilling her hot tea on the offending hand the third time he'd tried it. Finally, he'd removed his hand from her leg. Not making a fourth attempt, which she was grateful for.

Elissa should've taken that behavior as a sign and gotten out of the car. But no. She'd wanted to do Gretchen a solid. So, against her better judgement, she gave the creep another chance.

Idiota, her grandmother's voice echoed in her brain again.

The old woman had loved her. Elissa knew that without a doubt. She'd raised her after her own parents had passed on in a tragic automobile accident when Elissa was just twelve.

Her grandmother was a no-nonsense kind of lady who dished out priceless wisdom with brutally honest insights. It was the same way she dished out huge bowls of pasta with her amazing meatballs and homemade sauce. Not to mention a side order of back-breaking hugs that Elissa still missed.

Nonna cooked like that all the time. She made a huge pot of sauce every weekend, and she was happy to serve it to Elissa and her teammates and friends, especially after games and tournaments.

Soccer had been her sport of choice, and cooking had soon become her favorite hobby. Her grandmother had encouraged her in both pursuits. Guiding her in one and cheering her on in the other. Elissa still missed her terribly.

"Hey babe, ain't you gonna eat nothin'? You know they charge twenty dollars just to sit down," Little Gianni interrupted her train of thought.

Elissa was forced to turn her mind back to the present, which unfortunately included watching, *and hearing*, him as he sucked on his teeth and stuffed another breaded shrimp down his throat.

"I'm fine," she answered with a polite smile plastered on her face.

Just get home, Lissa. Just get him to take you home.

Elissa closed her eyes when he looked back down at his dish. Thank God for small favors, she mused. At least he was more interested in eating at the moment.

He'd taken her to the rattiest looking hotel and casino she'd ever seen in her life. And the buffet room?

Ew.

Seriously, the place had to be violating at least a dozen health codes. When Gianni had said Atlantic City, she'd thought at least the atmosphere would be exciting. But they were so far from the real glitz and entertainment, they might as well be anywhere else.

She sighed, looking at the plate she'd made for herself. Elissa couldn't even fake an interest in the food. As a chef, it was hard enough to dine out.

She was always judging the food, the service, the ingredients. How could she not? It was her business. And that was when the food was good!

This was not good. Not at all.

She'd been to hospitals that served better food. Old yellow lights buzzed and blinked around the buffet, giving it an abandoned kind of feel. The menu was made up of mostly frozen then fried or baked cuisine.

Reheated actually. It was like a giant TV dinner buffet where every item was previously frozen when already cooked and warmed up in an oven.

It was the kind of food sold cheap at restaurant

supply stores in bulk. Yeah, this was much worse than hospital food, in her opinion.

There was a worn carpet on the floor, a handful of scattered tables in the dining room, elevator music on in the background, and the entire place smelled like canned soup.

Not to mention not one of the five people there besides them was under sixty years old.

"Gianni," she said, leaning forward so as not to hurt his feelings.

"I thought you mentioned something about seeing a show tonight. Is it here?"

Please don't be here.

If he was taking her somewhere else, she could beg off and hire a cab to take her home. There was no way she was sitting through anything else with this man. Not now. Not ever.

"Ah, I see, babe, you want some entertainment first, I get it," he snickered loudly, and she blanched.

Whatever he thought was going to happen wasn't. She needed to disabuse him of the notion, and fast.

"Alright, alright. Lemme finish this, babe. Then we'll go up to the room I got for us," he said.

Before she could make sense of the ludicrous statement, he slurped another fried shrimp, don't ask how. Then he grabbed her arm and yanked her from the seat before she could even react.

Elissa tugged on his hold, but the man was immovable. Tossing a five-dollar bill on the table, Little Gianni snatched a toothpick from the hostess stand before dragging her outside.

Great, he was a cheap tipper, too.

All she wanted was to go home. Figuring the best way to do that would probably be to get him to the car, she let him lead the way.

Once inside, she would ask him to drive back to Hoboken so she could wring Gretchen's neck. Fuming, she pulled her arm out of his hand and walked behind him.

The rain was really pouring, and the cheap bastard had refused valet. Elissa ducked her head so she wouldn't get so wet. Of course, the jacket she'd brought was light and had no hood.

Gianni had an umbrella, but he didn't offer to hold it for her, and honestly, she did not relish the idea of getting any closer to him than necessary.

Seriously, not happening.

Now all she had to do was break the news. She had no intention of watching a show or returning to the hotel with him.

What could go wrong?

Excerpt from Grizzly Lover

"Resa," Oliver fisted the note he'd found tucked under the secondhand keyboard he'd just finished paying off.

The instrument sat against one wall of the cramped room, right beside the only window in the small Brooklyn Heights apartment he'd been renting the past six months since he came to the city.

For a Grizzly Bear Shifter used to the wilds of the woods as his backyard, it was quite the change, but he just had to try to see if he could make a go of his music. Oliver had always been gifted with a good ear, but even as a cub, his mother had encouraged him to go and seek his destiny.

Brooklyn Heights was as close to Manhattan as he could afford with his meager savings, but what did money matter anyway? Especially when there was music to be written. The window faced the south brick wall of another small apartment complex identical to his.

It didn't matter what it looked like outside, as long as he was able to breathe some fresh air. At least on the fifth floor, it was somewhat fresher than the heavily congested streets below.

She was gone. His mind registered that fact as he took in the empty room. She'd left.

"No," he growled, and aimed his fist at the tiled counter top, cracking a few of the old ceramic squares in the process. Mrs. Goldstein, the landlady, would be pissed when she saw that.

Oliver's Bear roared inside of him and his heart contracted painfully in his chest. It was worse than being sucker punched by Thor his idiot cousin, who was as big and strong as his namesake. Why would Teresa say such cruel things? He couldn't believe it, couldn't fathom his sweet Resa saying such foul callous words about their relationship. He read the hated missive one more time.

Oliver,

It was fun while it lasted, but even you can't be so naïve as to think I could find true love with a nobody. I just wanted to get back at my father. Don't bother looking for me or calling, I will have already changed my number.

Teresa

Yes, it was her handwriting. He closed his eyes on the wave of anguish that washed over him. Gasping, he sunk to his knees while the beast inside of him roared and sTimped his massive claws in fury.

Mate, his Bear cried out, but Oliver refused to answer his other half.

How could she just leave him like this? He'd been so sure of her, of them. He was positive that she loved him too. Being with her was everything to him. She was his fated mate. It was the first time he had ever tasted happiness. A taste that was bitter now that he knew it was all one-sided.

The first time he'd seen the golden-haired beauty, Oliver's Grizzly Bear had stood up and taken notice. The second he'd breathed in her peaches and cream scent, his animal had roared one single word in his mind's eye that would change Oliver's life forever.

Mate.

Following his heart, he'd approached the soft spoken, elegantly dressed Teresa Witherspoon after spying her at the park day after day. She'd sit on one of the cleaner benches and read from a book of seventeenth century cavalier poets.

"You like Lovelace? Looking at you I pictured a Donne fan," Oliver said when he'd finally found the nerve to approach her.

"Spiritualist poetry doesn't appeal as much to me I guess. I like Lovelace and Suckling. They're fun and witty."

"But they're just trying to get in a girl's pants with their poetry. You approve?" he grinned.

"It's not so much the seduction that appeals to me, it's the living in the moment. Carpe diem and all that," she shrugged.

There was something so tragically sad about her that his heart had squeezed in his chest with longing. He'd wanted to make her smile. Heck, he even pretended to stumble in the grass, laid himself flat just to get her to walk over and touch him. And she had, put her soft, long hands right on him to see if he was alright. He'd stolen a kiss and had never looked back. Until now. The dream was over. She'd left him.

Oliver's Bear roared in his grief. That last night they were together, he'd told her the truth about what he was. The fact that there were more things in the world than she had ever imagined.

Oliver Pax had committed a most grievous sin against his Clan. He'd confessed to a normal, a human woman, that he was a Grizzly Bear Shifter.

It was allowed under certain circumstances, like when the woman in question was your fated mate. He'd thought she'd taken it well, after all, they'd made wild, passionate love immediately after. Hell, he'd been so caught up in the moment, he'd marked her with his bite, tying himself to her irrevocably, but now she was gone.

What would become of him? Would he go mad like so many other Shifters who'd lost their mates? He had heard the stories. The tales of broken matings and rogue Shifters who needed to be put down.

Oliver tipped the bottle of whiskey back emptying its fiery contents down his throat. Then he threw the hated thing across the room. Something about the muted violence of the act satisfied his animal's need for savagery. The Bear inside of him wanted to tear the whole world down, but maybe work would be a better outlet, he thought.

Oliver sat down at his banged-up keyboard and began to play. He poured out his bruised heart. Wrote lyrics and tied them together with a fairy tale as old as they come. The Beast of Brooklyn Heights was born that day. And the rest, as they say, was history.

About the Author

C.D. Gorri is a USA Today Bestselling author of steamy paranormal romance and urban fantasy. She is the creator of the Grazi Kelly Universe.

Join her mailing list here: https://www.cdgorri.com/newsletter

An avid reader with a profound love for books and literature, when she is not writing or taking care of her family, she can usually be found with a book or tablet in hand. C.D. lives in her home state of New Jersey where many of her characters or stories are based. Her tales are fast paced yet detailed with satisfying conclusions.

If you enjoy powerful heroines and loyal heroes who face relatable problems in supernatural settings, journey into the Grazi Kelly Universe today. You will find sassy, curvy heroines and sexy, love-driven heroes who find their HEAs between the pages. Werewolves, Bears, Dragons, Tigers, Witches, Romani, Lynxes, Foxes, Thunderbirds, Vampires, and many more Shifters and supernatural creatures dwell within her worlds. The most important thing is every mate in this universe is fated, loyal, and true lovers always get their happily ever afters.

Want to know how it all began? Enter the Grazi Kelly Universe with Wolf Moon: A Grazi Kelly Novel or pick up Charley's Christmas Wolf and dive into the Macconwood Pack Novel Series today.

For a complete list of C.D. Gorri's books visit her website here:

https://www.cdgorri.com/complete-book-list/

Thank you and happy reading!

del mare alla stella,
    C.D. Gorri

Follow C.D. Gorri here:
    http://www.cdgorri.com

https://www.facebook.com/Cdgorribooks

https://www.bookbub.com/authors/c-d-gorri

https://twitter.com/cgor22

https://instagram.com/cdgorri/

https://www.goodreads.com/cdgorri

https://www.tiktok.com/@cdgorriauthor